CINDER

SISTER WITCHES OF STORY COVE, BOOK 1

NYX HALLIWELL

Cinder, Sister Witches of Story Cove, Book 1

"Cinder!"

My sister's screech jolts me upright from my prone position under the workroom sink and I smack my forehead on the steel basin. "Ouch!"

A follow-up shriek and the sound of shattering glass in the showroom has me muttering to myself and wiping my wet hands on a rag. "Coming," I call, scuttling out from under the pipes. A bucket, half filled with dirty water and hair from the drainpipe, along with numerous fittings and tools, are scattered around my legs.

"It's one of your mice," Belle calls. "They're loose again!"

Technically, they aren't *my* mice, but I tend to have an assortment of small critters who take to me, like McAlister, my pigmy hedgehog. The orphaned mice babies are now bigger than he is and strong enough to return to the woods where I found them last month. I brought them in, always a sucker for hurt or abandoned animals, and my sister, Ruby, helped feed and nurture them like their missing mother would have if she were still around. Now, it's time for us return them to the forest behind our home.

Sliding the bucket filled with a tangle of Zelle's coppery hair out of the way, I get to my feet. McAlister, on the countertop, stirs from his nap. He's nocturnal but still loves to be in the thick of things around the shop.

Zelle doesn't wash her hair in this sink, and I suspect the mice have been busy building nests with it, especially since they're constantly escaping their enclosure.

In the showroom, I find Belle standing on a stool behind the cash register, a book in hand, as usual. Zelle, the sister who dropped a glass candle, is half sitting, half teetering on the edge of a display table, her weight threatening to topple it and a dozen stacked soap bars to the floor. Her outstretched legs wave in the air. "It ran behind the Magical Forest display!"

Rapunzel, known as Zelle, and Belle, are fraternal twins. Although they're not identical, they resemble each other enough that people who don't know them sometimes mix them up. Today, Zelle's spiky hair has pink tips on the ends and she's turned her twin's, a platinum blond.

Wiping a strand of hair from my forehead, I check

behind the display. This reveals nothing more than dust and a cobweb. I mentally note we're low on Midsummer Night's Dream candles, the shelf they're housed on in the antique display cabinet nearly bare.

I turn to my younger sisters, "He's gone. You can get down."

Neither moves, scanning the shop floor with their matching brown eyes. "Where'd he go?" Zelle asks, suspiciously eyeing a nearby table of our sparkling Unicorn candles.

"Probably back to the workroom and the nest of hair you left in the drain."

Her feet hit the floor and glass crunches under her boots. "My hair?"

Since her locks grow at an astronomical rate, she shaves her head each morning. The hair regrows down to the floor by nightfall.

She touches the spikes already growing out from her morning routine, the signature pink tips part of her magick. "I haven't done anything in there in days, and I certainly haven't left any hair behind."

One of the goals I have for this year is growing our family business, the Enchanted Candle & Soap Company. Sales are thriving for our handmade, small-batch soaps and candles, especially online, and we're ready to add a full line of body care products. But a building expansion costs money. Money we don't have.

The upside is that a bigger showroom, workspace, and storage area will allow Belle and Zelle to up their hours, maybe even come on full-time, which Ruby and I could sorely use. As it is, the twins have to hold extra jobs in town to help pay our bills and keep our nearly two-hundred-year-old home from falling down around us. Belle works next door at the bookstore; Zelle is a hairstylist at Kit Kat Hair and Nails, specializing in events such as weddings.

In Story Cove, there are lots of weddings, along with parties of every make and kind, and good ol' Southern gatherings. Funerals and wakes, even simple Sunday dinners, are turned into big occasions.

"I know," I admit to her. "It's the—"

At that moment, I see a flash of gray from the corner of my eye. My hand shoots out in that direction. "Freeze!"

The mouse—half in, half out of the fall display near the cash register—stops dead in his tracks but squeaks loud enough to raise the hair on the back of my neck. I use my magick to keep him frozen as I scoop up his tiny body and look him in the eyes. "You've been a very bad little mouse. I know you're feeling your oats and are ready to get back into the forest, so we'll round up your brothers and sisters today and take a little journey, okay?"

His eyes convey more than his diminutive body could, even if it wasn't paralyzed. I allow my magick to roll back enough so he can move his head. His whiskers twitch as we stare nose to nose at each other, but I sense he understands my words and is relieved to return to the area where he was born.

My cellphone jingles in my back pocket, a chime to alert me to an incoming email. I take the little wiggler and hold him close as I pull it out. Zelle goes to grab a broom and dustpan to sweep up the glass candle, and Belle slides off her stool.

"Who's that?" she asks.

As I peruse the short message, I cringe. "One of those guys from the dating app. CuddlyBear59. Jeez, who makes this stuff up?"

"You got a match?" She hustles to my side to lean over my shoulder and read it. "An invitation to go to the ball?" She nearly squeals with glee. It currently seems to be her goal in life to set me up with someone.

"That's a big fat no."

She dances away, as though she has a partner waltzing her around the shop floor. "Tiffany Starling! Isn't it romantic? I can't believe someone so famous has moved to town, and is throwing a ball at her mansion. It's all for a good cause, too. She's helping the local theater with a silent auction fundraiser since they're going to perform the stage production of *The Glass Slippers*. The lead actress, Bonnie, will be wearing the original shoes during the play!"

I've heard Belle and Ruby chattering about this the past few days, but I've ignored most of it. "That's nice," I say off-handedly, "but I'm not going, and I really wish you hadn't put me on Fairytale Love. It's embarrassing. Not one of the guys who's sent me an email is someone I would date. Not even if they were the last guy on earth."

Consternation burns in Belle's eyes and she stops her pretend dancing. "Couldn't you try, Cinder? Fairytale Love has made over a million successful matches worldwide so far, and they're growing every day. Give at least one guy a chance, please?"

Dating in Story Cove is no fairytale, let me tell you. Finding my Prince Charming and a happily-ever-after is about as likely as Belle going a day without reading a book, or Zelle not walking around with pink hair.

Glancing at the email again, I notice the signature. "Jason Bonners. CuddlyBear59 is the meat market guy?" Another cringe. "Sorry, no." I make a face, thinking of what he does as a butcher. "Yuck."

"You refuse to date everybody," she argues, the exasperation in her voice grating on my nerves. "You need to get out more."

Zelle returns, shooting me a smirk, but at least she doesn't jump in on the conversation. She sweeps up the broken glass and chunks of candle and I reply to the email with a, "thanks, no thanks" message.

I pocket the phone and pet the mouse. "I'm too busy here and working on the building expansion. I don't have time for a boyfriend, so let's put that on hold for now, okay?"

Belle ignores me and goes to the front door to flip the sign over. It's almost 9 a.m. and time to open. With one hand she shoos me off. "Go take care of your mouse."

"You'll remove my profile from the dating site app?"

"Later," she replies.

Our shop cat, Savannah, has another renegade mouse trapped by the tail under a furry white paw when I return to the back room. The Angora gives me a bored look with her mismatched colored eyes as I retrieve the tiny gray baby, and I thank her for not eating him. A yawn and a stretch before she goes to the old cookie jar we keep handy and begs for a treat.

"You're spoiled," I tell her, depositing the mice in a shoe box. She purrs as I give her a crunchy fish-shaped treat. She meows for a second, after inhaling that one, but I stand my ground and ignore her pleading attempts, nearly having to stuff my ears with cotton because of her loud, incessant meowing.

After McAlister and I round up the rest of the mouse family, I'm carrying the shoebox to the back door when Ruby enters.

I'm the oldest of the Sherwood sisters, then Ruby, followed by the twins. My sister has the darkest hair of all of us, but shares my fair looks and freckles.

She's dressed in her signature red cape, even though the September day is warming nicely, and carries a basket of fresh eggs. "Hey, the van is making a weird ticking noise again." Undoing the cape's ties, she shrugs it off. "I had to walk through the forest to Nonni and Poppi's this morning. Not that I mind the walk on such a beautiful day, but do you think you could look at it?"

Our delivery van needs a tune-up, and probably a

new timing belt. More expenses, and more of my time. "I'll work on it as soon as I can."

"Want me to scramble up eggs for your breakfast?"

"I'm relocating the mice back to the forest, but I haven't had any coffee yet and I'd kill for one of your mushroom omelets."

"You got it." She peeks in the container and wishes the little critters well before McAlister and I exit with them.

In the bird-song filled woods, fallen leaves crunch under foot. The air is clean and crisp and I cast a magick spell on the mice to keep them from becoming food for larger animals.

I'm a softy at heart, and I can't stand the idea of them dying. I know it's part of nature, but they're orphans, like my sisters and I, and I wish them well as they scamper off into the burrow that was their original home.

The mouse who scared Zelle and Belle gives me another nose twitch and lifts a paw as if to say 'thank you.' I return the wave and amble back to our stately gothic home on Main Street.

The sprawling two bottom floors and a huge attic belonged to our fourth great-grandmother in the early 1800s. What began as a single-level dwelling for her family, grew when she started the company in her thirties after her husband died. She raised their six kids on her own.

Through generations of women on my mom's side, the soap and candle products have proved to always be in demand, and continue to support our family. We stick by Grandma Eunice's rules and put a little magick into every bar of soap, every candle. Now, with our lotions, body butters, serums, and loose tea and spices, we're taking Enchanted to a whole new level. We're still limited, however, with space and money for ingredients.

After I've had my omelet and coffee, I gather my things from the drain cleaning. Belle rushes to me in the workroom. "There's someone here to see you," she says, adding with a wink, "he's really cute."

My non-existent dating life is going to be the highlight of her day, no matter what I do.

I put McAlister in his cage. "Who is it?"

She leans closer and lowers her voice in a conspiratorial whisper. "It's Tiffany's son!"

"Tiffany?"

"Tiffany Starling! Honestly, Cinder, weren't you listening earlier?"

I shrug, grabbing my pipe wrench, still damp from the morning's work. I need to clean my tools, toss out the slimy water, and make sure the drain pipe doesn't leak. Then it's on to the van. "Can't you wait on him?"

"He said he needs to speak directly to you."

Sighing, I stare at her, searching for the lie. She's trying to set me up with a guy, and will go to any length to do so. But there's no subterfuge in her gaze, only happy excitement.

Wiping my hands, I follow her out, pocketing the wrench in my worn tool belt. Zelle is redoing the display she disrupted earlier, and Savannah has taken up residence in a patch of sunlight on the floor. Belle's Pekingese, Jayne Eyre, sniffs at the pant leg of a guy about my age, standing in a shaft of the same bright sunlight coming through the front display window.

He's tall, wearing an expensive tweed jacket and dark slacks, his wheat blond hair casually tousled. A lock falls into his eyes as he examines one of the charcoal soap bars in our Blackbeard line of male soap and beard products.

"This is Cinder," Belle announces, and he turns from the display on the antique table with a big smile.

"Nice to meet you." He extends a hand, a pair of sapphire blue eyes making me catch my breath. "I hope I'm not bothering you,"—he glances at the tool belt—"but Mother wanted me to speak to you specifically. Something about a refill of peppermint lotion—body butter, I think she called it? You made a tin of it for her. She swears it reduces the swelling in her feet, and she needs to wear those famous shoes of hers this weekend. She needs a refill."

I hear the words, but can't seem to process them, his stunning eyes making my brain short-circuit. The air catches in my sternum and seems as frozen as the mouse was earlier.

He looks at me somewhat expectantly, and it takes great effort to make my brain cells function again. When his gaze travels to the tool belt once more, I feel a flush of heat spreading up my neck. I gingerly touch the wrench and then point a thumb over my shoulder to the workroom. "I, uh...had to fix a pipe."

"I see. It appears you're a woman of many talents."

I'm praying I don't have grease on my face.

"Yes, well..."

Peppermint Pigs is the name I've been toying with for my latest creation, a foot cream borne of my own need for it, as well as Nonni's. She has terrible swelling in her aging feet. I keep adding magick to my portion, hoping to shrink my giant ones.

So far, it refuses to reduce my size 10s, but I do have soft skin.

Belle and Ruby love the name, Zelle doesn't. The salve is made with beeswax and honey, along with peppermint and vanilla, and is specifically for soothing tired feet. I haven't added it to our line-up yet since it's still in the beta testing phase, and I simply don't have time to create dozens of tins of it.

Ideas I have plenty of. Time and money? Not so much.

I remember the woman who came in two weeks ago complaining about her feet. I knew right off the bat she wasn't native to Story Cove, but I had no idea she was the famous actress who recently moved to town. "That's your mother?" I stammer. "Tiffany Starling?"

He's still holding out a hand and Belle clears her throat, startling me out of my awkwardness. "Sorry," I say, reaching to take it. "I didn't realize who she was. I'm so glad my potion—um, body butter—worked."

The warmth and solidness of his hand makes me not want to let go. "You didn't recognize her?" He gives a chuckle. "Don't tell her that. Her ego would take it hard."

I still haven't released his hand and a silly grin breaks over my face. "It's our secret. Nice to meet you... I didn't catch your name."

A bemused expression crosses his face at my apparent ignorance about his family. "Henri Finch Starling. Friends call me Finn."

Finn. Nice. Everything about him is really nice.

"She told me this place had something special about it. Straight out of a children's storybook, she said." He glances around. "She was right. Is it on the register?"

"Register?"

He releases my hand. Reluctantly, I let him. "For historical homes?"

Probably should be, but making repairs to the old place or expanding it would have to meet their strict guidelines—and cost even more. "Afraid not."

"She's a beauty." He winks and my breath catches again. "I can see you're taking good care of her."

Trying to at least. I need several thousand dollars to get the bats out of the attic and update the electrical.

Someday. "I'm sorry I don't have any of the lotion your mom wants on hand at the moment. I'll have to make a fresh batch and deliver it later today."

Mentally, I add one more thing to my to-do list.

"That would be great." His grin broadens and he reaches inside his jacket, withdrawing a square ivory envelope, and handing it to me. "Mother would like to invite you to our fundraiser and ball this weekend."

I can feel Belle nearly squeal with excitement behind me. Even Zelle comes to attention. "Thank you, but's not necessary. I'm happy to make up the foot cream for your mother. It's no big deal."

His smile falls. "We'll pay for the lotion and delivery. This isn't in exchange for that."

"Oh, no, I understand. It's just...dancing isn't my thing."

He slowly returns the invitation to his pocket, his brows drawing down. "Sorry to hear that. You might still enjoy it, even if you don't want to dance. There's music and food, and the silent auction of my mother's memorabilia from the film."

I attempt to look interested, but I haven't even seen the movie. "I appreciate the offer, but—"

"Just think about it okay? Maybe I'll see you later. You know where we live right? On the hill?"

In Story Cove, that particular hill is referred to as Millionaires Row. Ms. Starling purchased Myth Manor, if memory of Belle's chattering about it serves.

"We know," she states from behind the counter. She's finishing up with a woman who's buying several candles from our Charming Crystals line, and eavesdropping on our conversation at the same time.

He nods at me, waves at Belle. "Again, nice to meet you. I hope to see you soon."

The customer exits on his heels, and Belle nearly grabs and shakes me, she's so frustrated. "I can't believe you didn't accept that invitation."

Zelle shakes her head. "Honestly, Cinder, I can't either. He's handsome, rich, and look how awesome he is, coming down here to get lotion for his mom's feet."

Handsome, rich, and nice...I'm not sure why I'm running away from that, but all I can do is shrug. "We only just met him," I say, thinking I should push Belle at him since she's so enamored with his mom and her movie.

He's perfect for her, and maybe if she had a boyfriend, she'd leave me alone.

With that idea in mind, I head back to work.

CHAPTER

TWO

That afternoon I have to fix the van before I can deliver Ms. Starling's order to Millionaires Row.

I look like a grease monkey by the time I'm done with the tune-up, but the van runs and that's good enough for now. The timing belt is still on my list, but I don't have time today to change it.

I clean up, taking extra time to get the grease out from under my nails, before I pull out the ingredients for Peppermint Pigs and go to work. Zelle's left for the hair salon for her regular afternoon appointments, and Belle is helping Ruby with the shop.

When she's not out front, Belle's in back reciting trivia about Tiffany and the movie that made the starlet famous. "She could sing, dance, act...you name it. You don't find many actresses like her anymore."

"That's nice." As Belle flutters around, I measure out ingredients, setting out several empty containers.

No point in making only one tin, and Ruby can take one of the extras to Nonni.

"I can't believe you didn't know who she was when she came in," Belle says. She's dressed in a blue skirt and white blouse, her hair in a bun on the top of her head. Jayne follows her every move as she inventories the glass containers we use for candles, but doesn't leave her comfy spot on the upholstered chair in the corner. "I sure wish I'd been here!"

"I don't watch many movies, and she was a star a long time ago," I reply in my defense.

"*The Glass Slippers* is a classic, not just because it won three Oscars, including Tiffany for Best Actress. They say the shoes in the film were cursed. The set too. Tiffany was only twenty-two when she did that movie."

She continues telling me about the film. The '80s blockbuster features a down-and-out waitress, Katie, who believes her mother is a famous actress in Hollywood. Left as a baby on the steps of a church with nothing but a pair of high heels that resemble some worn by said actress in a film, she has no family. At eighteen, Katie treks across the country in the shoes, sure they'll bring her good luck. Along the way, she faces challenges and has help from several fairy godmother-type women.

Measuring the shea butter into the mixer, I shrug. Having lived a somewhat dramatic family life, I'm not keen on watching someone else's, even if it is fiction. "I prefer sci-fi over that kind of sappy stuff."

"It's a coming of age story," Belle insists, as if this should change my mind. "The synchronistic events, especially when Katie arrives in Hollywood where she lands a starring role in a film *with* the actress she believes is her mother...I mean come on, it's so perfect."

"I thought the actress *wasn't* her mother in the end."

Belle whirls on me. "Yes, but all the women along the way that helped Katie...*they* mothered her. She learns it doesn't matter if you're related by blood, it's what's in the heart that creates family."

My sister, the romantic. Since she was only fourteen when we lost our mother, I can't blame her for loving a movie with that theme. "Maybe I'll have to watch it this weekend."

Her eyes light up. "I'll join you! You know, Katie meets and marries a handsome prince in the movie. It's really a happy ending."

Of course she does. Hollywood at its finest. I struggle not to roll my eyes as I switch the mixer on. Slowly, I add the vitamin E, honey, and essential oils. "What is this about a curse?"

Belle leans on the table, her eyes big as she gets out her cellphone and taps at the keys. When she finds what she wants, she turns the phone to show me pictures of people I don't recognize but understand were part of the movie.

"During and after the filming, strange things happened on the set. People came down with odd diseases or had accidents. Two died. They filmed the first couple of scenes a few miles from here, but the set burned down. Put the film on hold for months, and then they returned to L.A. and did it there. Rumor spread that the set and the props were cursed, including the infamous shoes. All of the people who got sick or died either worked on or wore them. From what I understand, that only added to the movie's success, but still, can you imagine?"

Not really. "Tiffany seems fine and she's over sixty, right?"

"True, and she still has the shoes. Maybe she's immune to the curse?"

"Do you think she'll auction them at the fundraiser this weekend?"

Belle shakes her head. "She would never get rid of those shoes. Those are her lucky charms. She said so herself a million times in interviews. You know, Callie Lane was originally cast for the role, but she tripped in the shoes and broke her ankle."

She scrolls, then flashes a woman's picture at me. "That's why the role went to Tiffany, and the rest, as they say, is history."

Belle twists around and returns to her inventorying, the *bing bong* of the shop bell over the door a steady background noise.

"Did Callie ever return to acting?" I ask out of curiosity.

"Oh sure," Belle answers. "She starred in a couple

of movies later on, but never received the fame Tiffany did."

Once the mixer is done, I scoop the mixture into the three containers, and sprinkle a touch of healing magick over them before I stick on labels and screw on the lids. "Ms. Starling seems nice, and maybe now that she's moved to town and likes our products, we'll see an increase in business. Her endorsement of my foot cream could bring in tons of business."

Belle shifts several glass containers out of her way and reaches into the back to pull out more. "I so hope we can expand the shop like you want, Cinder. But I also hope you'll find more time for yourself. I'm not sure how that can happen when you're so busy you can barely breathe."

"You let me worry about that." Being the eldest, I feel a responsibility to keep our business going and keep our family together. Mom and Dad would want that. "I'm fine."

While I'm cleaning out the mixer, our godmother, Matilda, strolls by with the wave of a hand, the tips of her handkerchief dress fluttering around her ankles. "I'm here," she says, as if our world has suddenly become brighter because of her. "By the way, Odin is hanging upside down from the ash tree again."

"Uncle Odin," Belle scolds under her breath, even though he's not within earshot. "What's bugging him now?"

"Maybe he needs a few minutes of peace," I defend.

At times, I'd like to join him out there in his contemplative hanging. He longs for the old country, the old way of life, and a realm filled with magick. Since magick is as natural to us as brushing our teeth, I wonder what it'd be like to live in that realm. He's a gentle, wise soul, who appreciates the poetry books Belle brings him, and has a special fondness for Ruby's raven familiar, Lenore. "I'll check on him before I take this to Ms. Starling."

"Ms. Starling?" Matilda whirls on me. "The movie star?"

Where has she been? Maybe she's been tuning Belle out like I have. "Don't tell me," I say, washing my hands. "You're a fan of *The Glass Slippers*?"

She squeezes into the nearby upholstered chair with Jayne, thunking her Pegasus stainless steel travel mug on the side table. The dog gives a snort, not appreciating the invasion, but she's too lazy to get up and move.

Matilda sinks into the sliver of upholstery with a dramatic sigh that might give Ms. Starling a run for her Oscar-winning money. "Of course I am. Have you seen that movie? It's all about feminine empowerment."

Our godmother might have once been a Valkyrie. She's never confirmed it, but there are strong hints she lived in a land of ultra-empowered women. No surprise she enjoys movies with that theme.

Today her hair is woven into multiple long braids interspersed with sparkling crystals and tiny feathers. The bohemian earrings dangling by her neck are also filled with crystals. She's wearing enough makeup for all four of us, and she has stacks of bracelets on both arms. Her feet are bare, as usual, from her earthing activities outside.

She claims the Pegasus mug is filled with a magick potion to help her get her powers back—the ones she lost years ago to an evil witch who lives a couple towns over. My sisters and I are more prone to believe it's filled with alcohol. Strong alcohol.

"I have to go," Belle says, checking the big metal clock on the wall. "Daisy isn't feeling great today and I told her I'd come in early to take over. We're expecting a new shipment of books."

"Does she need some tea?" I ask.

"Good idea." Belle gives me a look that tells me Daisy, the owner of the bookshop, is fine. My sister simply doesn't want to hang out with Matilda. "I'll grab a container of our white tea and ginger for her on my way out."

"I could do a healing charm," Matilda offers.

"No," we both answer in unison.

"What?" Our godmother gives us a chiding look. "I'll be careful."

The last charm she performed ended up turning a customer into a toad. I'm not sure Belle's aging boss could handle that.

"I'll watch the movie this weekend," I say as a diversion, hastily scratching out an invoice for Ms. Starling. "Meantime, I need to run this to my famous customer. I'll be back in a few minutes."

Matilda jumps up from the chair. "Can I go with you?"

I sense impending disaster. *Divert!* Matilda's brand of crazy isn't for everyone, and I'm not ready to have this opportunity with Tiffany and her son destroyed before it has a chance to actually start. "It's not a social call, and I'll be right back. I have a ton of work to do. Besides, Ruby may need your help."

As if on cue, the sister in question calls from out front. "SOS. Can someone grab the register?"

I look at my godmother and sister and raise a brow. "See?"

Belle rushes past me. "You're so psychic. Don't forget to be nice to Finn. You really should accept that invitation to the ball."

Matilda crosses her arms over her chest. "You received an invite to the ball? Why didn't you tell me?"

Talk about potential disaster. Matilda in a mansion filled with normal people? I don't need to be psychic to know that's a horrible idea. We might end up with a zoo. "I declined it graciously. I'm not going to anything that requires formal wear and pointless socializing."

She looks at me as if *I'm* the crazy one. "Blessed Fates, why not?"

"I have nothing to wear, and I don't know how to dance. Isn't that what they do at these things?"

Her purple irises darken, and I nearly take a step back, afraid of the lightning that occasionally shoots from her fingertips when she's agitated. "Deliver the foot cream. We'll talk about this later."

I don't want to talk about it later, but I'm glad to escape. After checking that Uncle Odin is okay, I drive the van, worn out timing belt and all, up to Millionaires Row.

CHAPTER

THREE

Myth Manor is truly enchanting. I can only guess at how many square feet of luxury are contained inside the historic mansion, once owned by the town founder. The palatial stone walls hold a host of juicy stories as well, I bet, since Myth Manor is rumored to be haunted.

I've never paid much attention to local scuttlebutt, but now I wonder if I'll see or sense any ghosts. That's more Ruby's ability than mine, but on occasion, I get hits.

I have to pass through a gate and a security guard to get on the ten-acre property, admiring the mermaid water fountain centered in the grand circular driveway. The landscaping alone is probably worth more than we make in a year.

If only...

Sometimes I let myself dream about winning the lottery, how I'd fix up our grand old mansion and keep my sisters and I together. Our place is nothing like this one, but if we had one tenth of the wealth Ms. Starling appears to, we'd be set.

I find myself straightening my shirt and I brush at a spot on my jeans as I stand in front of the large, double-door entrance. A fall swag hangs on it, miniature pumpkins and fake fall leaves glistening in the afternoon sun.

I ring the doorbell and am promptly greeted by a woman, who doesn't seem surprised by my appearance. She ushers me inside, her name, Rowena, stitched into her pale blue dress.

As I start to say who I am and why I'm there, another woman rushes in and interrupts.

"Callie," she says, introducing herself. Rowena turns away and disappears. "Come in, come in. Finn said you'd be by."

I follow her across the dark marble foyer, taking in the double chandeliers over our heads. Twin staircases leading to the second floor are done in plush white carpeting and dark wood railings. "I really can't stay," I tell her. "I just came by to drop this off for Ms. Starling."

She's dressed in a red blazer, gray skirt, and conservative black heels. She appears to be about the same age as Tiffany, and has her permed hair teased to great heights. There's more gray than blond in it, yet it's blended to perfection. I bet Zelle would be impressed.

"Wait, did you say Callie? As in Callie Lane?"

She ushers me into an immense sitting room, complete with a variety of elegant antiques, built-in bookshelves, and a large telescope at the rear window overlooking the valley. Her smile is ingratiating. "I'm surprised you know who I am."

I wouldn't if Belle hadn't talked about her. She's aged considerably from the photo my sister showed me. "You're a friend of Ms. Starling's?"

She carries a small notebook and taps it with a pen. "I'm her assistant." Then she looks slightly abashed and adds, "And her friend, of course. We've known each other a long, long time."

She shows me to a vintage upholstered sofa. I'm guessing it's a replica. A fire burns in a giant stone fireplace, the mantle decorated with more pumpkins and a leaf garland. Another woman enters, this one bigger and gruffer, with dark eyes and dressed in a white apron. She carries a tray of tea and miniature cookies that she sets on the coffee table.

"Tea?" she asks.

Callie keeps moving. "I'll let Tiffany know you're here."

As she leaves, the woman serving us pours tea into a china cup and shoves it at me before I can answer her. She doesn't ask if I want sugar or cream, even though both are on the silver tray, and she pours a second cup, placing it across from me. Without another word, she turns and leaves as well. A moment later, I hear voices in the hall and Callie and Ms. Starling enter the room.

When Tiffany came into the Enchanted Candle & Soap Company two weeks ago, she was in pearls and satin. Today, she's dressed in a long, flowing dress with a plunging neckline, and a feather boa draped across her shoulders. Diamonds sparkle at her neck and ears.

I stand, ready to give her the lotion and get out, but she greets me with air kisses like we're old friends. Motioning me to sit, she snatches up two cookies, and takes the extra teacup, then sinks into the chair.

"I'm so excited for this weekend," she exclaims. "I can't wait for you to see the play. Your sisters too. Finn tells me you have several. I'm sorry I didn't get to meet them when I visited your store the other day."

She goes on like this for a few minutes, not allowing me to get a word in edgewise. When she finally comes up for air to devour a cookie and drink her tea, I slide the tin and invoice across the table. "It's great about the fundraiser to help the theater company. And the town is all abuzz about the ball. I'm sure it will be a big hit." I think about Finn and his smile. "It was nice to meet your son. He seems like a great guy."

She shuffles her feet to the side, pointing to the shoes she's wearing. "He takes great care of me, and now that I have your special lotion to keep the swelling down in my feet, I'll be wearing these babies as much as I can. This is what people really want to see...the glass slippers."

I hadn't realized these were movie shoes. I make

admiring sounds as she continues to talk. Callie scribbles notes on her pad, occasionally looking over at the fire as though she's heard all of this a million times. As I glance at the shoes again, my second sight kicks in and I notice the high heels give off a weird pale yellow aura.

Maybe they're cursed like Belle is convinced of, or they're just a size too small for Tiffany's feet these days. The skin is puffy and mottled around the edges where she's crammed into them.

Someone clears their throat from the doorway and I shift over to see a woman in khakis and a flannel shirt. Heavyset, she wears cat eye glasses with a beaded string on them and looks down her nose at me before shifting her attention to Tiffany. "You wanted to see me?"

Tiffany waves her in, then says to Callie out of the corner of her mouth, "Will you get me a martini? I need something stronger."

Callie rises, seeming neutral about the whole thing, almost on autopilot, as if she's taken requests and filled Tiffany's desires for so many years, it's second nature. As she exits, the woman in flannel moves closer, but doesn't offer to sit. Sweat lines her forehead and she eyes the cookies before withdrawing a handheld digital recorder from a pants pocket. "Are we doing an interview now? Is this a pertinent person in the biography?"

Her accent is upper Northeast, possibly New York or New Jersey.

"Oh no." Tiffany waves her off. "I wanted to introduce you to my new friend, Cinder. She's the one with the amazing shop filled with great smelling candles and soaps. You have to try her foot cream! It works miracles on my cankles and swollen feet. Might help yours too. I can order you some. Cinder, this is Janice."

I can't help my gaze dropping to the woman's feet. Her black leather flats are worn on the outsides where her feet run over.

The assistant tips her head to look through the bottom of her glasses at me again. "Janice DuBois," she reiterates. She glances at Tiffany, her breathing noisy as if she's run a mile. "Karl...from Acquisitions... phoned." She has to inhale between every couple of words. "He wants you to...call him back...right away."

Tiffany jumps up as if something bit her. "The publisher is doing a biography on me and that's why Janice is here," she says with a dramatic flourish of her hand toward the woman. "Can you believe it? *Me*. I guess with all this attention about the play, the ball, and the fundraiser, I've generated enough interest to get a book deal. They're claiming my fans will go nuts for it. I can hardly wait! And if Karl is calling, you know what that means!"

She's beaming, but Janice seems slightly annoyed. I have no idea who Karl is or what it means.

Wiping sweat from her face, Janice fills me in. "There's a possible...movie remake...on the table." She switches to Tiffany. "You better not...keep him waiting."

"Right!" A triumphant clap of hands that jangles her diamond bracelets. "Strike while the iron's hot!"

Tiffany excuses herself, telling me she hopes to see me at the play.

Janice walks out without saying goodbye, one chubby hand massaging her chest. I'm left alone with the tea and cookies. I stand and glance around, then snag a cookie. They're good—a lemon sugar blend that melts instantly on my tongue. I suspect home-made by the woman in the apron.

Long minutes pass and I'm about to sneak out the front door, hoping I can get back to work, when Finn arrives in the hall, cutting off my retreat. "Cinder," he says as if thrilled to see me. His deep voice sends a delightful shiver down my spine. "I didn't know you were here."

Light streaming through a second story window shines down on us in the foyer, like a spotlight. The tweed jacket is gone, a casual blue polo showing off his broad chest and intensifying his eyes. He's shoeless and I see bright colored socks on his feet. This makes me feel warm and fuzzy inside since I have a collection of unique and interesting pairs myself.

"I was just on my way out," I say, self-conscious about the heat rising in my face. "I dropped off the foot cream, and your mother was gracious enough to offer tea and cookies, but I really have to get back to the shop."

He grins. "I'm afraid I can't let you leave until you accept our invitation to the ball. Otherwise, I might have to make an excuse to visit your shop again just so I can see you."

The warm feeling grows. "I bet you say that to all the girls."

"Not true." He chuckles and the sound echoes inside my chest. "There's a dinner for the play's cast on Thursday night. It'd be great if you and your sisters would attend as our guests. Really, it's the least Mother and I can do."

"I don't know. Blackmailing me into accept the invitation is pretty low."

His eyes spark with humor. He accepts my kidding with another smile, showing off his perfect teeth. "My desperation is showing. I don't know anyone here, so I'm claiming you as a friend. May I walk you out?"

An elderly fellow approaches us, his skin tanned and wrinkled, garden gloves on his hands. The smell of soil and fresh air drifts from him. "Mr. Finn, I sure hate to bother you." He gives me a nod, acknowledging me before continuing. "I need help with two giant topiaries your mother wants brought into the atrium. Gotta repot them before the ball, and now's the only time I have to do it."

Finn steps toward the front door. "I'll be there in a minute, Jackson."

"I'll just show myself out," I tell Finn. "You go ahead."

Before either of us can move, Ms. Starling rushes in, all smiles. "Oh, Finn, there you are, Rowena's having a fit about stringing the lights in the atrium.

We need the topiaries at the entrance to anchor them, and she can't do that until they're repotted. Be a dear and help Jackson move them in for me?"

I swear, she bats her lashes. He gives her a placating smile and turns to me with an apology in his eyes. "Raincheck?"

"Of course."

He and the gardener leave, and Tiffany grabs my hand, pulling me close. "Good news, my agent's working out a deal for the remake. I'm so over the moon about all of this, I can hardly stand it."

"Congratulations."

"I feel your lotion already working on my feet, too."

Glancing down, I see she's switched to a pair of fuzzy slippers.

"Let's have a tour of the mansion, shall we? I'm not done refurnishing it, but I want you to see the strides we've made. Callie's been such a help. She did the cinema room to resemble a classic theater, complete with gold gilding, tiered seating, and box facades!"

I try to get away, but she won't hear of it. She takes me through two wings of the house, showing me her awards, photographs from her long career, and an assortment of gifts she's received from fellow actors, politicians, and world leaders. We pass a large commercial kitchen, delicious smells drifting from it, and go down a long, dark hall to the home theater. When we emerge, she takes me to see attached atrium at the rear of the mansion.

I don't see any ghosts on the tour, but the decades of families living here has left a definite residual energy. Rowena and Callie flit by here and there, and I admit I keep an eye out for Finn.

"I've always wanted one of these," she says, leading me inside in the enormous atrium.

The heat and humidity of the greenhouse hit me square in the face, and the smell of blooming flowers, mixed with garden soil, tickles my nose. As we stroll past rows of plants, she goes on and on about a rare orchid she had shipped in. "Tiffany Blue, it's called," she says with a happy sigh as she shows it to me. "Of course, I had to have it as the centerpiece for my baby."

The orchid's blue coloring is quite breathtaking, especially with a spotlight shining on it. "It's beautiful," I admit.

There are a number of impressive plants, and she claims more are on their way, that she wants to fill the atrium with exotic plants, birds, and butterflies. It will be a sight when she's done, complete with a huge waterfall in the center.

Again, I can't help comparing what she has with what my sisters and I do. Still, I'm grateful for my family, even my whacko godmother and odd uncle.

"Does Finn live with you, then?" I ask.

"I wish! He has a darling place in Atlanta. It's one of the reasons I moved back to Georgia, so I could be closer to him. Callie and the staff were horrified when I told them we were moving here. It's quite a change from L.A., you know. But I've transferred my charity business here, and I think everyone is transitioning well. It's so good to see my boy. He's only here for a few days to help me settle in, but I plan to convince him to stay longer."

"That would be nice," I find myself saying.

As we round one of the enormous displays, she pulls up short and her face turns grim. "Oh, dear."

I follow her gaze and feel my insides turn over. Oh dear is right.

On the floor in front of us, a bag of potting mix is dumped on its side. Face down next to it, with her glasses askew on the side of her face, is the biographer, Janice.

I rush to shake her, but she doesn't respond. As I check for a pulse, I realize she's wearing Tiffany's shoes.

There's no time to wonder how that came about, no time to save her either. She's without a pulse, and the blank look in her half-open eyes makes my stomach drop.

Janice is dead.

FOUR

I have a thing about shoes. Not like millions of women who hoard them, including my sister Zelle, but an odd magickal gift that allows me to literally step into someone else's and get psychic hits about them.

The mansion is buzzing with police after my dialing 911 and contending with Tiffany having an anxiety attack. The glass slippers are still on Janice's feet, and the coroner has zipped her into a black bag. As they wheel her through the house and out the front door, I'm stuck in the sitting room with cold tea and stale cookies, not to mention Tiffany, Callie, Elsa Shores, the apron-wearing chef, a housekeeper named Rowena Appleton, and the gardener, Jackson Reeves.

My cousin, Robyn Wood, is a detective on the Story Cove police department. She oversees the removal of the body and comes in to talk to us. Finn's voice filters into the room from the hall, as he gives his account to one of the uniformed officers.

Robyn has already questioned Tiffany and taken her statement, and I didn't have much to add as we were together when we found Janice. As Ms. Starling chugs a martini with shaking hands, speaking quietly to Callie, Robyn tells Rowena she'll be back for her in a moment.

I stare out the window as the ambulance pulls away, no lights flashing, followed by the coroner's dark van. I overhear Callie say to Tiffany, "Why was she wearing the shoes?"

Tiffany sets down her glass on the fireplace mantel, decorated with pumpkins and gourds. "How should I know? I took them off while I was on the phone with Karl, and I set them in the ballroom for the silent auction." This is interesting information, since it sounds like she *was* going to put them up for auction. Belle will have a fit, wanting to buy them.

She toys with her glass, clasping and releasing it. "Janice must have put them on before she went to the atrium."

"Why would she be out there?" Callie wants to know, almost sounding angry.

I hear a dramatic sigh and I glance over my shoulder at the two women. Tiffany wipes a hand across her forehead and pushes a stray hair away. Her diamond ring winks under the light. "She liked the flowers, why else? She said so the other day. They were simple, undemanding, and she could breathe easier in there. Rowena told me she went out there every day to think."

Callie's lips firm. She sounds unconvinced. "More like she was trying to get away from all of us. I saw her on her phone constantly in there. She never even looked at the flowers."

Ms. Starling doesn't argue, as if it's too much trouble. "They found her phone a few feet away from the body. It appears as if she tripped and fell while talking to someone. She probably went to the atrium for privacy."

Tiffany grabs her drink, upending the glass to get the last bits of alcohol as she stalks out. I watch her go, Elsa pacing nearby. Callie looks at us, her stressed expression intense, then follows Ms. Starling with a heavy sigh.

"Why Story Cove?" I ask the housekeeper once they've vanished into the recesses of the mansion.

Rowena sits in the chair Tiffany occupied earlier. Hands in her lap, her fingers worry each other. She peeks up at me. "What?"

"Why did Ms. Starling decide to move to Story Cove? Was it only to be closer to Finn?"

She glances at the fireplace, the fire long extinguished. Her voice is soft and hesitant. "This is where the magic happened. It started her career."

"What magick?"

I'm thinking of actual supernatural magick, but apparently Rowena is talking about the glamour and magnetism of times past.

"They filmed the first few scenes here, didn't you know? That's why the theater is doing a reproduction of *The Glass Slippers* for the fortieth anniversary. Ms. Starling has been trying to reclaim that magic, as she calls it, from the beginning of her career." She glances around the room and lowers her voice. "I think she believes being back here will give her a second chance at fame."

"In the movies?"

She shrugs, the straps of her white apron tightening before her shoulders droop and the left strap falls. "Georgia does have a strong film industry, but she might look to the theater. She can work out the kinks with your local group and then who knows? Take it to Broadway?"

"You mean as the director or something?"

"Yes, and I might get the part of Katie!" Rowena stands and moves to the window, her face growing excited. "She's been going over the lines with me daily. Just between you and me, I think she wants to play Cassandra."

I really have to watch that movie soon, because I have no idea who she's referring to. "Who's that?"

Rowena looks at me as if I'm dense. "The woman my character, Katie, believes is her mother, who really isn't, but you know."

I'm not great at math, but Ms. Starling's age seems to be an issue. "How old is Cassandra in the film?"

A shrug. "Well, you know, they can do a lot with makeup and lighting."

Elsa guffaws. "The character is in her early forties! Starling can't pull that off."

Rowena frowns at the chef. "Ms. S. looks really young for her age."

It's been four decades, and I remember Belle stating Tiffany was twenty-two at the time of the original film. She *does* appear younger than early sixties, but I doubt she can pull off the role of a forty-year-old. Maybe she's planning on rewriting the script to her advantage?

I shift the subject. "Have you worked for her long?"

Rowena shakes her head. "Not quite a year."

I study her profile. "Do you like it?"

She meets my eyes and smiles. "Oh yes, although…"

"What?"

A resigned exhale. "I'd hoped she'd help me get a part while we were still in L.A."

The girl's disappointment twists her features, even though she's trying to hide it. "Georgia's not exactly a hotspot for the film industry, is it?"

She offers a sad smile. "No."

"I bet Ms. Starling is glad you came with her."

"I am too. She's a bit melodramatic, but I always dreamed of being an actress, so I understand how that is. Life is a stage."

Robyn interrupts, asking Rowena to come with her to give her statement. I move away from the window, my stomach growling since its nearing my dinner time and I missed lunch.

"This is crazy about Janice, isn't it?" I ask Elsa.

She crosses her arms over her apron and I detect the slightest German accent I failed to notice before. "She was a bottom feeder. Who knows what she was up to out in the greenhouse?"

"I thought she went out there to have privacy for a call?"

"Because she couldn't find privacy elsewhere in this giant mansion?" Elsa sneers toward the hall. "Ms. Starling has been acting ridiculous about all of this, and that DuBois character wasn't helping. All this drama over a pair of stupid shoes."

"Janice looked like she was having trouble breathing when I met her."

"She was eating me out of house and home! On some weird diet, always demanding her food cooked in a certain manner. I couldn't wait for her to leave."

Elsa whirls away, and I go back to staring out the bay window, my mind churning.

Minutes later, Rowena returns. "This is certainly going to put a damper on Ms. Starling's return to the spotlight," she says, worrying her hands.

At the fireplace, poking the burning logs, Elsa harrumphs. "The only thing it's going to endanger is the biography, and knowing Ms. Starling, she'll twist this to her advantage and come out smelling like roses."

"Good." Rowena's voice is stronger, but I notice she takes a step away from Elsa. "Her biography will be a bestseller, and all of her fans will be thrilled to read it."

Finn enters, crossing to my side. "I'm so sorry about all of this."

"It's not your fault, but I am as well. How's your mom?"

He leads me away from the others. "She's a trooper. Detective Wood said that you're free to go. Would you like me to take you home?"

A giddiness stirs in my chest. He's kind and thoughtful, but right now, under his blue-eyed gaze, I feel how upset he is. "No need to. You stay with your mom and make sure she's okay. I'll see myself out."

He walks me to the front door, take my arm as we dodge all the extra folks. We pass Robyn, speaking to a coworker. "Tell your sisters 'hi,'" she calls to me, and I assure her I will.

Finn sees me to my van, and thanks me again for delivering the body butter to his mother. I doubt she cares much about it at the moment. "Will she get her shoes back?" I ask.

As the sun is setting, it shoots peach and pink colored rays across the beautiful lawn and drive. I notice he's still shoeless, his bright socks, like peacock feathers, contribute to the colorful setting. "As far as I know. There's no foul play." His mother is definitely a product of Hollywood, but Finn sounds like a Southern gentleman through and through as he continues. "Mom is still having a fit. If she doesn't get those shoes back, she'll be cussing a blue streak."

I climb into the driver's seat and put the key in the ignition. "That's understandable. They're an important item with the play, fundraiser, and ball."

We say our goodbyes and I head home. When I get there, driving to the small rear parking lot, I find McAlister on the back porch cleaning his face. "What are you doing out here?" I scold him. I sit on the top step and he comes over, climbing into my lap.

Ruby rushes out the back door, having sensed my presence. "Cinder! We heard about a woman dying at the mansion. Are you okay?"

I'm still shook up—it's not every day you find a dead body—but I put on a cheerful face. "It was crazy, but I'm fine."

I rise and we enter the house. Starting this month, we have extended hours that run through the holidays. It's nearing closing time, and the shop has a steady stream of customers checking out the pumpkin soufflé soaps, pumpkin spice candles, and assorted apple scented products. Fall brings out something in folks that makes them want to explore their connection to scent and candlelight, as well as comforting things like tea and soup.

"I'm glad you're okay," Ruby tells me. "What happened?"

As we walk past the storeroom, I hear the door chime bonging constantly with people entering and exiting. "I'll tell you about it as soon as we close. Who's on the register?"

"Belle, and Zelle is on the showroom floor assisting customers."

By morning, the whole town will have heard the news, and that may bring a few curiosity seekers in. There's really not much to tell, but I have a feeling I'll be repeating my experience more than a few times.

Forty-five minutes later, the last customer leaves with her arms loaded, we've closed out the cash register, and we climb the stairs to the second floor where our living quarters reside. Ruby has homemade mushroom and orzo soup slow cooking on the stove and pulls out bowls to begin dishing it up.

Belle sets the table, her twin putting the kettle on to boil. I beg off for a few minutes to run to the bathroom and wash my pale face. I stare at myself in the mirror over the sink, trying to shake the memory of Janice lying on the atrium floor.

My freckles stand out on my pale face, my eyes shadowed. I can still smell the bag of potting soil that was spilled next to her, see her twisted glasses. Worse, her blank stare seems branded into my brain.

When I re-enter the kitchen, my sisters are all seated, and Uncle Odin and Matilda are there as well. Savannah munches her dinner from her food bowl, flicking her tail. I take my place at the table, take a long sip of the hot tea, and then, as we begin our meal, I launch into the story.

When I'm done, I field questions, and having barely touched my soup, I dig in. I mention Elsa and Rowena discussing Janice, as well as Ms. Starling, and the fact Elsa seemed irritated and annoyed by both women.

Zelle reaches for a roll from the breadbasket. Her hair is down to her knees, now in a thick braid. "Too bad you can't get your hands on those shoes."

A shiver tickles down my spine. "I kept picking up a strange sensation from them."

"What kind of sensation?" Matilda asks.

"I'm not sure. Could be my imagination, but it was a weird vibe. I mean, they're beautiful and all. Sparkly and obviously made for the big screen, but there's an aura about them. I couldn't tell if it was positive or not."

Belle nods as if this makes perfect sense to her. "The curse."

"Maybe," I admit. "If there's some kind of magick on them, it's not obvious, though."

Uncle Odin, who's been pretty quiet through this whole thing, scratches his white beard. "Is it possible the shoes are truly cursed, my dear? Do you think that's why Janice put them on in the first place? Perhaps she was enthralled."

I think about it as I sip my tea. I feel calmer now, more detached about what happened, although there's a sticky sadness in my chest for Janice. At least, my logical brain can sort through the events better.

Janice was there doing a job, and a somewhat glamorous one at that considering she was writing the biography of a famous movie star. Not exactly dangerous by any means. "It didn't feel like that type of energy," I attempt to explain. "It seemed defensive, almost wary. Very...guarded. Probably because it didn't want me poking at it. Robyn seems positive it was nothing more than an accident."

Belle eyes me across the table, a knowingness in her gaze. "I bet our entire inventory of Once Upon A Time candles it wasn't."

Belle lives in the world of books, both fiction and non. They literally talk to her—it's her witchy power. I hate to disagree, and the tingle under my breastbone tells me she may be right, so I keep silent. "Well, it's too bad it had to happen. I only met the woman for a brief moment, but what a shock. Ms. Starling was very upset by the whole thing, and for good reason."

We finish our meal and clean up. Later, in my room, I cuddle with McAlister, but every time I attempt sleep, all I can see is the blank look in Janice's eyes.

CHAPTER

FIVE

As expected, the town is abuzz the next day with the news that Ms. Starling's biographer is dead.

Throughout the day people stop by and try to talk to me about what happened. Robyn comes in shortly after lunch to let me know she's ordering an autopsy. Even though she believes it was an accident, possibly even a heart attack, Janice's family is in an uproar and want it confirmed.

This is the most excitement Story Cove has had in a while, and I get the feeling Robyn wants to make sure she is as thorough as possible. Since it involves a famous movie star who's recently moved to town, Robyn needs every t crossed, and i dotted.

That afternoon, I'm making a batch of our popular Pumpkin Waffles candles. I measure the soy wax flakes into my aluminum pot and place it on the burner. While that heats, I measure out the spicy scent, enjoying the top note of buttery pecans, the pumpkin and warm cinnamon middle notes, and the sweet vanilla and maple base. It fills me with a sense of calm.

Matilda ambles in, wearing one of her wild gypsy outfits, complete with a sparkling headband, and boosts herself up on the counter, feet dangling over the side. She's in my way, but I say nothing, working around her as I label jars and place wicks in them.

I'm not sure yet if she's having a good or a bad day, and it's best to know that before you say the wrong thing and set her off. "Did you just get up?" I ask, then cringe, because this innocuous question in and of itself may be the wrong thing.

She drinks from her mug, and eyes me over the edge. "For your information, I was at the farm this morning, helping Nonni harvest the last of her basil and mint."

This is good. Matilda and our paternal grand-mother don't often get along, and Nonni can use all the assistance she can get with her garden. "That's great. I'm sure she appreciated the help."

Matilda looks at her nails with no small amount of disgust. "Now I have to have Zelle give me a manicure."

At least she's not attempting to do it herself. She likes to use magick to turn her nails all shades of the rainbow. When it's wonky, our walls and ceilings end up that way too. "She'll be happy to do so."

Matilda sniffs the air. "I do love that scent. Brings back memories of your mom making breakfast."

A pang of longing hits my heart. I stir the soy chips as they begin to melt. "People are already thinking about Thanksgiving, and asking for this candle, so I figured I'd better make up a big batch."

"Did you get any sleep last night?"

My godmother stares at me from her lofty position. I pull the backing from the sticky tabs for the wicks and begin centering them in the jars. "Not much."

"It's not every day you stumble across a dead body, huh?"

Is she reading my mind? One attribute about Matilda is she never cuts corners or skirts difficult subjects. She puts it right in your face so you're forced to deal with it. The good thing is, she stays with you while you do. "I can't get that last image of her out of my mind."

"Do you really think those shoes are cursed?"

I shake my head, stir the melting wax again and check the temperature. One hundred and sixty-eight degrees. A little more to go.

I line the jars in rows like soldiers on the countertop, their long wicks flying in the air. "I thought about it a lot last night, and I don't feel like they're cursed, but there *is* something off about them. Something magickal for sure."

She gathers the wick holders and begins dropping them over the wicks, the metal making a flat *clang* on the glass jars. I remove the soy from the burner, the perfect temp now, and add the pumpkin waffle scent, stirring it absentmindedly.

Those shoes. What is it about the famous pair?

Sure wish I could stick my big size 10s in them.

Like it's not enough my unique magickal skill is in my tootsies...I have to contend with Bigfoot feet. I bet Ms. Starling is more like a size 7, 8 at the most.

I understand her connection to them. Just like certain trinkets, souvenirs, and other memorabilia, shoes can hold memories and people's energy. I've sensed anxiety coming from a pair of wedges when the owner was late for work, or happiness blooming from dress heels when the woman was dancing. Their experiences and emotions can bleed from the very fabric of their footwear when I slip them on.

Adding a tiny amount of orange coloring to the batch, I stir. Buried deep in my closet is the last pair of shoes my mother wore. Every once in a while, I pull them out and put them on, feeling her happiness from that night, that weekend. She and Dad went away for a second honeymoon, Matilda watching us four girls. The night they were on their way home, she wore the shoes she'd married Dad in. She'd taken them for that second-honeymoon weekend because they held so much joy and happiness for her.

Our parents were killed in a car accident that night, and although I don't know her last thoughts, the shoes still hold the joy of that special time and her deep abiding love for my dad. I can't imagine losing the shoes, and hence, that connection to her.

Absorbed in my thoughts, I'm waiting for the wax to cool enough to pour. I lean back against the opposite counter, watching the gauge.

Matilda seems to understand where my thoughts have gone, and she gently tries to pull me back. "What do you think about this ball that Starling is throwing? Will she still have it?"

"I don't know. Seems like a huge event to her, and the town is sure excited. From what she said yesterday, she was working on invites. That was before we found the body, of course."

"Maybe she'll postpone it for a week or two."

"That would make sense. She wants the ball and fundraiser to be all about this theater production of her movie. If she has the ball now, it'll be overshadowed by Janice's death."

Matilda takes another sip of her magick potion and doesn't comment. She hoists herself off the counter. "I think Odin and I should go together when it happens. Check this woman out."

I'm scared what might happen if Matilda decides she doesn't like Ms. Starling. "I don't have an invite for you."

A shrug and a daring grin. "Crashing parties isn't my style, but I have ways of getting into them. It *is* my job to look after you girls."

Gods above. "We're in trouble then," I tease.

A dishtowel sails at my face and I dodge it, laughing.

"I hear her son's a real looker." She winks at me.

For all her faults, my godmother is a good sport when I need it. "Yes, he's quite handsome. He could star in movies himself. But before you get onboard with the others to hook me up with someone, we're just friends."

"Whatever you say, Cinder."

She leaves with another wink, and I begin pouring the candles. Once that's complete, I move them to the table to cool, and as I'm cleaning my pitcher and spoon, Ruby sticks her head in the door. "You have a visitor."

"Who is it?" My sister knows pretty much everyone in town, so if she's not telling me who's asking for me, I can only guess it's someone I don't want to talk to.

She grins wickedly and disappears, leaving me to sigh, stick my candle making supplies in the sink, and head to the front.

Finn is standing near the register, something in his hands. His face lights up when he sees me and he holds out the item like an offering. "Mother had Elsa make this for you and your sisters. She'd like all of you to come to the cast dinner on Friday night, and she'd like to purchase gift bags for all the attendees. Gift bags with your products in them. There's going to be around fifteen guests, plus she wants one for Callie and the staff too. The cast from the theater production will be there, along with the director, and a couple other patrons of the theater."

I accept the package and see a wrapped coffee

cake. It's still warm, and the smell of cinnamon and apple drifts up from it. I haven't had breakfast, and my stomach delights in the idea of having a slice. "Wow, thank you. This smells delicious."

A customer enters and Ruby winks at me behind Finn's back as she goes to wait on them.

"It's the least we could do after what happened yesterday," he tells me.

"How is she doing, your mom?"

"She feels horrible about it." He reaches inside his coat pocket, withdrawing a piece of paper. "Thank goodness you were with her when she came across Janice. I don't know how she would have handled it on her own."

She was a hot mess, so in a way, I'm glad I was there as well. "She's going through with the theatre production, I take it?"

He nods and hands me the paper. "Here's a list of who will be attending the dinner. You certainly know the majority of them better than we do, so I hope it won't be difficult to figure out what products will appeal to them. Cost is no issue, so feel free to fill them up."

I accept the list and glance over it. He's right, I know most of the folks. "Thank you. This is a great help."

"Do you guys live above the shop?"

As two women enter, I motion for him to follow me to the workroom where we can chat out of the way of the shoppers. "Yes, one of our maternal great-grandmothers started the company in the early 1800s. It's stayed in the family, and my sisters and I love it."

We stand in the doorway between the showroom and the workroom, and he nods. "I bet it has a lot of cool history. From the outside, it looks like a mix of Gothic and Greek Revival. That turret is really something."

"You know your architecture."

"I have a thing for it, and also a degree. My specialty is BIM."

"Sorry?"

He looks slightly abashed. "Building Integration Modeling. Think of it as 3D architecture. Mostly, I only get to use it for new projects, but I have a love of this historic stuff and have used it for several historic homes to bring them into this century without destroying their integrity."

That's pretty cool. "So you're not just the spoiled son of a famous movie star?"

He takes the dig with good humor. "I stay as far away from Hollywood as possible."

"And your dad?"

He looks thoughtful for a moment before he answers. "Dad has never been in the picture."

Touchy subject, then, best left alone. The two women are looking over at us, coy smiles and flirty body language directed at Finn. I feel annoyance buzzing under my skin.

"This is a small town in Georgia," I tell him as a warning. "It won't be long before everything about you has been discussed over coffee at the diner. Anything you believe is private may eventually come out."

He turns from the gawking women, scanning the work area. His voice lowers. "Understood. Trust me, there's not much about Mother's life that hasn't been splashed across the tabloids at one point or another. Mine not as much since I stay out of all that chaos, but when they need gossip, they'll dig for anything."

I don't read tabloids or follow Hollywood scandals, so I don't know specifically what he's talking about. Still, I can guess. "I'm sure you have a thick skin and are used to it, I just wanted you to know that you're big news in this town. Everyone wants to know everything about you and your mom, and now, with this unexpected accident, things might be intense for a while. Do you think she'll postpone the ball?"

His chuckle is edged with awkwardness. "Are you kidding? She's been looking forward to this for months. It's not like she and Janice were good friends. Truly unfortunate, what happened, and yes, she's upset, but she knows how to spin everything."

He says this with a bit of disappointment.

One of the women boldly walks over to us. "Are you Finn Starling?" She sticks out her hand without waiting for him to reply. "I'm Amelia Longsten, head of the PTA, and head of the Chamber of Commerce. I own the Red Rooster, two blocks over. Best breakfast and lunch in town."

Finn, not having seen her approach, automictically

pastes on a neutral smile and shakes her hand. "Nice to meet you."

Amelia's voice drips with her honeyed Southern accent. "I heard all about what happened at the mansion yesterday. Your mother must be *so* upset. Please send her my regards." She pulls a business card from her purse and hands it to him. "And I hope you'll both come and eat at my place soon."

Amelia is twice divorced, and on the hunt for her next husband. A part of me feels slightly protective of Finn, and that takes me by surprise.

I only want to make sure she doesn't try to take advantage of him. That's what I tell myself as she literally giggles under her breath and walks away.

"The hunter is on the prowl," I murmur.

"Nothing new for me, unfortunately." Finn turns, focusing on the workroom. "Is this where you create your products?"

He knows it is, but I get his drift—he'd like to get out of Amelia's line of sight.

"Let me show you." I usher him into the back and shut the door between the rooms, hoping Ruby can handle the customers on her own.

"Thank you," he says, relief relaxing his face. "It's not that I don't want to meet people, but..."

"No worries. I get it." Waving a hand at the room, I do my best Vanna White impression. "This is where the magick happens."

Literally.

He zeroes in on the candles curing on the table,

leans over them and takes a big sniff. "These smell amazing, like I want to eat them."

I laugh. "Good, that's the idea. These are our famous Pumpkin Waffle candles. It's one of our top three sellers in the fall, along with Caramel Apple and Autumn Stroll."

"Sounds as delicious as it smells. Business is good?"

"It is, but it can always be better. If I could expand the shop as well as this workroom, we could double our business in the coming year."

He rubs a finger and thumb along his chin, thinking it over. "Why haven't you?"

I sigh, setting the coffee cake on the countertop, the list next to it. "Expansion takes money and time. I can do the work myself to save on expenses, but I need to find time and a significant amount of cash to get started. It'll happen, I have to be patient."

I show him more, including our soap molds and the area where we dry herbs for the teas and spices. We peek in the storeroom, so he can see the inventory shelves and equipment.

"Have you considered taking on an investor or a bank loan? That could provide startup capital for the expansion, and you no doubt have equity in the house and business."

"We stick to paying for improvements and repairs as we go, like our grandmother did back in the day. No loans. Investors particularly like to have a say in operations, and there's no way my sisters will go for that."

"Understood. You might still be able to find a silent partner, one who doesn't care about control and would be willing to invest the initial working cash. In return, they'd merely want to see a return on investment within a certain timeframe."

No interest? Not likely. "That *would* be magick. Unfortunately, business relationships like that are hard to come by here. I'll give it some thought, though. Thanks for the advice."

"I'm happy to pay for the gift bags now if you like."

I wave him off when he reaches for his wallet. "I'll bring the bill the night of the dinner."

His eyebrows lift. "You'll come then, and stay?"

"If my sisters find out you invited us and I didn't tell them, I'll never hear the end of it. We'll be there."

As I see him to the door, he's smiling, and after he leaves, I find I am too.

That night, I can't sleep again, and McAlister and I go downstairs to work on the list.

I line up an assortment of gift bags, dividing them between the men and the women who will be at the cast dinner. Then I head into the shop and begin picking out travel size samples of various soaps, candles, bath bombs and sugar scrubs.

The bath and body section is one of the areas I know we can grow, and quickly. At this time, we have a set of products we offer year-round, but the specialty items and seasonal varieties we could offer are endless. Like the foot cream I took to Ms. Starling, I can see a whole line of therapeutic lotions.

As I'm setting out the multitude of options, Ruby stumbles in, rubbing her eyes and yawning. Lenore caws and flies in behind her, landing on the birch branch perch I installed years ago for her. "Need help?"

"Nah. I can't sleep and figured I might as well make myself useful."

She scratches McAlister under his chin as he runs among the tiny samples, stopping at a small container of sugar scrub to pick it up and toss it around. Being nocturnal, he's delighted to have us up and busy.

Ruby glances at the list. "I couldn't sleep either. Might as well join you." Lenore squawks, her beady eyes taking in the full table, as well as McAlister. In response, he drops the sample, curls in a ball, and shows his spines.

Ruby grabs a stool and pulls it up. "Do you want me to make herbal tea?"

"Might as well. This will take some time."

She leaves and I grab a couple more products, using a bit of magick to inform me what several of the guests might like since I don't know them well. The magick sparkles as it leaves my fingers, floating around in tiny waves, the energy stopping and hovering over different items. I thank it and collect those products, hauling handfuls back to the work table.

McAlister is now standing on all fours, making noises in the back of his throat at Lenore. She appears to ignore him, cleaning her feathers. Savannah's here now, too, lying on a half-empty shelf and yawning.

Ruby waves a hand over our cups, releasing a sprinkling of magick that I assume is to help us sleep, before she hands one to me. The tea is the perfect temp, and I sip, feeling my tightly strung nerves settle. "Thank you."

She squeezes my arm and sips her own brew, chuckling at McAlister, doing somersaults on the table and rooting around in a bag he toppled over.

Belle and Zelle enter, arm in arm. "What's up?" Zelle asks.

"Work, what else?" Belle supplies, knowing me well.

Ruby sets down her cup. "Did we wake you?"

Belle shakes her head and they disengage. "I can't stop thinking about the ball. Zelle and I were discussing what Cinder should wear."

"I'm not going to the ball. Belle, you should take my place. I can talk to Finn tomorrow and ask him about it."

She huffs with indignation. "Don't be ridiculous. While I'd give my magick to attend, I'm not taking your place."

This is a surprising statement since she loves her magickal gift as much as breathing.

"You're going," she continues, sneaking a sip of Ruby's tea, "and we will figure out one way or the other how to get you there."

Jayne strolls in. Dashing past her, Zelle's ferret familiar, Rumpelstiltskin, is equally happy we're up. The two settle into the dog bed Belle has under the table, but pretty soon, the ferret is running around like a demon, creating chaos.

At least it gets Belle to quit talking about the ball.

She goes to our tiny office and returns with an armful of books. As Zelle help sort through the products I've gathered and begins dropping them into the gift bags, Belle flashes the covers at us.

"I found a dozen biographies that Janice Dubois wrote, all of them making the New York Times bestseller list, and all about famous—and a few *infamous*—people. Several were unauthorized, and from what I read online, she had powerful enemies because of them."

I glance at them, seeing pictures of well-known men and woman. A rock star, a sports mogul, a former governor, and a married couple who supposedly worked for the CIA.

Belle sits in the corner chair, Lenore squawking from overhead, and scrolls through stuff on her phone. "Some of the lesser knowns include a guy who snitched on a big chemical company, the former mayor of Georgia, and two actors who ended up in jail or rehab."

"Did Tiffany pick her to write the biography?" Ruby asks.

I'm not sure why it matters. "Probably the publisher, don't you think?" I direct this at Belle since she knows more about books and the writing world than the rest of us.

She's secretly writing herself, a romance, I believe, but she hasn't told any of us yet. My intuition picked up on it, and I don't want to call her out. She'll reveal her dream to us when she's ready.

A nod at my question as she continues to scan what's on her phone. "In this article it claims she's had death threats over a couple of the unauthorized stories. One of them was from a mafia guy, and the publisher eventually pulled the book from the shelves, because not only was Janice in danger, people in the editing and marketing groups were as well."

I see Janice's face again, her lifeless body. Setting down a soap, I fight a sudden bout of queasiness. "Who would think that you could merely trip and kill yourself?"

We all exchange a look, and something feels off about all of it. In my sisters eyes, I see they're feeling it too.

"Maybe it was a heart attack." I nod. "She was breathing hard that day, and I saw her rub her chest when she left."

Zelle finishes with a bag and puts her hand on her hip. "There must be plenty of biographers out there that Tiffany could have picked, regardless of what the publisher wanted. Seems odd that she went with someone like Janice."

Belle stands and slips in next to me and picks up the soap I laid down. She places it in the bag I was working on. "Janice hasn't published anything in the last five years, since the mafia guy's death threats. Maybe she was looking for a comeback like Ms. Starling."

We finish the bags and I take them to our back

door loading area while the others clean up. When I return, I hear a knock at the front door.

Ruby and I exchange a glance. "Who could that be at this hour?" she asks.

The knock sounds again.

Robyn is on the other side when I get there, and she waves through the glass window. I unlock the door and let her in, my sisters forming a semi-circle around us.

"Hey, I'm sorry to bother you guys this late, but I saw the lights on."

"No problem. What's up?" I ask.

She tugs her green jacket closer, as if chilled from the fall night outside, or maybe from what she's about to tell us. "I thought you'd want to know—the coroner did a rush on the initial autopsy."

She glances around at the four of us, before her gaze comes back to me.

An icy sensation runs over my bones. "And?"

"Janice Dubois didn't trip and die," she says. "And it wasn't a heart attack."

None of us so much as breathe.

"What was it?" I dare to ask.

Robyn shakes her head in sad disdain. "The poor woman was poisoned."

The next morning, we're all bleary eyed and moving slow, even though Ruby's herbal tea helped sooth my nerves so I could sleep.

Before Robyn left, she pulled me aside and asked me to be her eyes and ears at the mansion. To stay close to Finn and Tiffany, see what I can uncover. Any clues might help her determine if there's a killer on the loose.

When I come to breakfast, I find Matilda and Odin laughing over scrambled eggs. Ruby's at the stove, and she makes me sit. Zelle has a big day at the beauty shop, she says on her way through the kitchen, grabbing a piece of toast, and Belle is working at the bookstore.

I sip strong coffee, eat without really tasting the eggs, and think over what Robyn told us.

She couldn't share all the details about the investigation, now a possible homicide, but has a hunch the poison may have been in something Janice ate or drank. She was on several medications for high blood pressure, and the substance may have interacted poorly with them.

Thank goodness it wasn't in the tea or cookies, or more of us might have died. Robyn wouldn't come out and say it, but she doesn't believe it was an accident. Why would someone want to kill Janice? That's the question of the day, and the handful of people that were at the mansion when it happened narrows down the suspects.

Except for the fact, as Belle pointed out last night, she had powerful enemies outside of Story Cove.

So if it was intentional... I call up memories of that day in more detail, before Janice died, and rifle through them. Tiffany, Callie, Finn. Elsa, Rowena, the gardener.

And me.

We were all there, and the timeline of who came and went and who spoke to who is mixed up in my brain.

After breakfast, Ruby rushes down to open the shop, and I join her, restocking shelves and losing myself in work. Customers come and go, and I help a few choose various products. My heart isn't in it, though, and finally Ruby shoos me off to the workroom.

I find Matilda in the chair, watching an old sitcom. She's brought Uncle Odin's tiny white TV from his room and set it up for her enjoyment.

"Could you help Ruby for a few hours?" I ask.

Her gaze slips over to me before returning to her show. "I'm kind of busy here."

I think about casting a spell on her, hauling her up from that chair and forcing her out to the shop floor. Burying that image, I paste on a smile. "You're so good with the customers," I lie. "People ask for you, and I hate to tell them all the time that you're not here."

Her eyes, complete with inch-long false lashes, swing back to my face. She sits forward, and I sense her quirky magick scanning to see if I'm pulling one over on her. "People ask for me?"

Not really, but playing on her ego usually gets her to do what I want. I fortify my defenses against her magick, more worried about it backfiring and turning me into a dragon or something, than her realizing I'm not being truthful. "All the time. You have fans, Matilda. You should give them what they want once in a while."

She stands, gestures at the TV, shutting it off with a snap of her fingers. I tense, waiting for it to explode, but it doesn't. Uncle Odin has probably protected it from her.

"What are you going to do?" She straightens the long lacy tunic she's wearing over a vibrant green skirt. Sans shoes of course.

"I want to look at the building footprint and figure out how to turn at least twelve square feet of the workroom into extra shop space." I motion toward the street. "We already have a decent window for more display space to draw customers in, but the flooring will have to go and I need to assess how to widen this doorway so they can easily pass through."

Caught up in my dream, I go on about removing the wall between the work and storage areas and designing a better layout of the storeroom shelves.

When I turn back, it's apparent I've bored Matilda to death, and she has gratefully fled to the shop to help Ruby. *Score.*

I like working with my hands, whether it's mechanical or structural. I can't say I actually enjoy plumbing, but it's not that hard, just messy. Keeping the van running, fixing little things around the shop and our home, brings me satisfaction. I try to be both Mom and Dad at the same time, running this place as smoothly as possible. Mom was the dreamer and Dad was the handyman. They were good with finances and strategic planning. I like to believe I've inherited the best of both of them.

Doing everything as well as they did isn't easy considering I'm just one person, and they were both pretty amazing. I do my best, and I feel their presence around me, as if offering their support.

The worktable is on castors, so I flip the brakes up and begin shoving on the heavy table. I unload several shelving units filled with supplies for soap making, taking the items to the storeroom. After shifting bags of ingredients out of the way, I take bunches of dried herbs and spices off their hooks and put them upstairs in the kitchen.

Although we keep the place as clean as possible, dust flies, and I have to wipe things down. I sneeze when I get some up my nose, and once I'm done with what I can move on my own, I find McAlister sleeping in his cage in my room, and bring him down for a few minutes of playtime.

He's used to the normal layout and has to inspect the changes. I give him a few of his toys to play with and I continue visualizing how I can blow out the wall here and put a different one there. In my mind, I imagine how the front area of the workroom will be transformed into the shop, seeing my lotions, body butters, lip balms, and body scrubs filling shelves and being displayed on antique tables.

One of the equipment shelves was in front of an old fireplace that's no longer usable. I have to take the shelf apart in order to move it, but once I do, I'm able to fully see the old hearth. Because of what was in front of it, it's full of cobwebs, and no surprise, the mice built a nest here.

Long thick strands of Zelle's hair, mixed in with what appears to be cotton, twigs, and feathers, are stuffed in amongst a few old logs. The feathers are long and black, and I assume they're Lenore's.

I'm growing tired, my muscles fatigued, and I glance around to make sure no one's watching. I wiggle my fingers and send magick into the hearth to clean it out. The hair, twigs, and logs come to life, rising into the air.

The bucket I used to clean out the plumbing

becomes the recipient of the mouse nest, along with the rest. Once I haul that outside, I begin scrubbing the inside of the hearth, coating myself in soot and ash and more things I'd rather not think about.

The fireplace will make an excellent focal display, and will be a beautiful addition to the atmosphere at Christmas time, if we put a gas log in it and fix the mantle. As I'm running my fingers around to make sure the chimney flue is closed, I stumble upon a metal latch.

It's cool to the touch and doesn't feel like the damper lever. It's bigger and seems to have ornate ridges. As I fiddle with it, a door on my left cracks open with a spine-tingling groan.

My heart jumps. I pause, eyeing the slender crack, and wonder what I've just discovered.

Grabbing a flashlight from the storeroom, I rush back and get down on my knees once more. With another reluctant groan, the door opens fully when I shove at it.

Stale air clogs my nose. The flashlight beam bounces off stone and metal, revealing a winding staircase that leads up.

The turret! I believed it was simply a decorative addition to the house, lending an air of mystery to the place, but none of us ever found an entry to it. We always figured it was one of those architectural constructs added through the decades that had no function.

I'm debating whether to take the stairs, when Belle asks from behind me, "Cinder? What are you doing?"

I back out of the hearth and wipe cobwebs from my face. She must be here on her lunch break. "I'm not sure what I just discovered, but it looks like the entrance to the turret on the side of the house."

"A secret room?" Her eyes light up. "Are you kidding me?"

"Fun, huh?"

"I knew there had to be a way to get in there."

"Apparently, I found it." I offer the flashlight and she bends down to look through the open door. "Be careful. We have no idea if that structure is stable, or what we might find."

She sits back on her haunches and gives me a pointed stare. "A door hidden in the fireplace that leads to what must be a secret room that our great-whatever-times-grandmother built all those years ago? You really want me to proceed with caution right now?"

"Yes, I do. Whatever is up there might have been sealed up for a reason and we have no idea what it is. Who knows what we might find?"

She does an exaggerated eyeroll, and for a moment, I feel like a mother chastising her daughter about safety. "I hear something." Her head tilts as she listens. "Books! I hear books!"

Then she vanishes up the staircase.

Cursing under my breath, I run to retrieve a second flashlight, then crawl through the door to the stairwell. It curves, so I can't see her anymore, although her beam illuminates the stone walls.

An actual castle-like turret. I'm flabbergasted, but Belle's excitement is seeping into my bones. The stairs creek and groan as I climb. "Belle?"

"Hurry, Cinder! You won't believe it!"

My breath comes fast, not because of the steep ascent, but due to the elation in her voice. At the top is a landing and a circular room laid out before us. Belle sweeps her light over bookshelves lining the walls. Dust specks float in the air, flashing as my beam illuminates the space. It falls on a desk with ornate legs. A low-backed chair with delicate spindles and a deep, ruby-red velvet seat looks as though the owner dashed off in a hurry, expecting to return shortly.

I sneeze, the dust particles scattering and more rising. Belle begins pulling books from the shelves. "Oh my," she says flashing her light across the titles. "Look at these, stuck here all this time."

The desk beckons, stacks of papers, brittle with age, a feathered ink pen, glass jars of dark liquid long dried, and what looks to be recipes, lie in a tumbled mess on top of it. In one corner is a sepia photograph of a woman in front of the store in a long skirt, buttoned-up blouse, and a hat.

Grandma Eunice. I study the grainy picture, seeing a hint of us in her eyes, the slope of her nose. The turret is there.

My nose tickles and another sneeze sends a stack of papers flying. I collect them and find most are soap recipes. With each one there are interesting ingredients that we don't put in our current versions.

"Eunice, you little witch," I chuckle under my breath.

Belle looks up from reading. "What is it?"

"Our grandmother was adding charms and spells to her soaps," I tell Belle.

She rushes to the desk, eyeing the recipes with me, arms filled with books. "I love her even more," she says and we both laugh.

"We better see if Ruby can summon her." Ruby's mediumship skills are somewhat unreliable, mostly I think because she doesn't use them often, but there have been a few times when she's connected with our ancestors. Even Mom and Dad.

Boy, that made me happy.

A few hours later, Belle is behind the register, and Ruby and I are in the secret room. "There's a whole set of her journals." She carefully turns pages in a leather-bound book, excitement in her voice echoing around me. "I can't wait to read them."

"Can they help you connect with her?"

She hugs one to her chest. "Worth a try, right?"

"Tonight after closing, when everyone's here, let's try it. I'd love for her to know we found this place, and I'd also like to know why it got closed off and the only way to access it is through the fireplace."

"For sure." Ruby grabs another journal, but eyes a larger book next to it. "Cursed Objects...this might come in handy for you right now."

She passes it to me and I flip through a few pages. "I'll look at it before bed."

At the desk, she studies the photo. "Maybe Eunice had the same rare ability you do and that's where you inherited it."

My shoe-reading gift is such an oddity. "Anything's possible, I guess. Some types of magick do pass through the generations, but as far as I know no one has ever had this particular one."

Ruby considers it to be cool. "I know you don't like to tell people about it, but you might mention it to Robyn. She could let you try on the shoes. Maybe you could tell who murdered Janice."

The idea of seeing Janice's last moments sends a shudder through me, and I'm doubtful I would get that information, since she was poisoned. She probably didn't know until it was too late.

"I'll think about it. What I pick up on is so random, and those would be more likely to show me something about Ms. Starling rather than Janice."

Ruby shrugs and we start down the steps, her bringing the book and journals. "You're right. But I sure would like to get my hands on those shoes and check them out."

I make a face even though I'm ahead of her and she can't see me. "Really? Why?"

"The Glass Slippers? Are you kidding? Those are one famous pair of footwear."

Famous or not, I still wonder if they're cursed.

CHAPTER

EIGHT

Robyn informs me she plans to re-interview everyone, since it seems the poison was ingested, and the unusual compound found in Janice's stomach had to be sent to an independent lab for identification.

Whatever it is, it may have had a reaction with Janice's medications, and at this point, the police are not sure if she ingested it accidentally, or if someone poisoned her.

The idea that she might have been murdered clangs around in my head the rest of the day. While I didn't know the woman, I feel a desperate need to find the truth.

After dinner, Uncle Odin, Matilda, and the four of us sisters gather in the dining room. We light candles, hold hands, and Ruby reaches out to the other side of the veil to attempt contact with Eunice.

One of our great-grandmother's journals, along

with her photograph, are centered on the table. An icy sensation runs over my skin as Ruby calls on her. McAlister, in my pocket, jumps out and scampers away.

Chicken.

Lenore rests on the back of a chair, squawking and flapping her wings every few minutes. I know she's channeling magick to assist Ruby, but the ruckus grates on my nerves.

Unfortunately for me, it's not Grandma who whispers in my ear. It's the voice of a much more recently departed individual.

"What's going on?" Janice asks. "I feel so...light."

"Eep!" I nearly knock over the table when I jump. My family stares at me, but all I can do is scan the room.

The candles flicker. I can't see a ghost, but the air is so cold, my breath frosts. "Janice?"

Ruby leans toward me, voice low. "*The* Janice? She's here?"

I give a quick nod. "Don't you hear her?"

Ruby, and everyone else, shakes their heads.

Great. Guess this is my chance to find out the truth about what happened. "Janice, I hate to tell you this, but you, uh...died. At Ms. Starling's."

"*Died?*" she screeches. The candle closest to me blows out. "That can't be true. I'm...fine. Why is it so dark in here?"

This is going to be harder than I expected. "You're not fine, Janice. I'm sorry. You were poisoned.

The day I visited Myth Manor...do you remember that?"

There's a long pause. "What a drama queen."

Her non-answer makes me shift gears. "Ms. Starling?"

"Those cursed shoes," she mutters. "All that hubbub about them. On and on and on..."

"Ask her who killed her," Belle whispers urgently.

I lower my voice as well. "She doesn't even realize she's dead."

"I'm not dead!" Janice yells and the remaining candles snuff out, plunging us into darkness.

By the time we relight them, she's gone, and no one wants to continue searching for Grandma Eunice at this point. "See if you can get her back," Zelle says to Ruby.

"She didn't come because of me. It's Cinder who has that connection."

She mentioned a drama queen and the shoes, but nothing that tells me how she ended up poisoned. I rub at a wax dripping. "Do you think I can get her back to answer more questions?"

Ruby shrugs. "You can try."

We repeat what we were doing to call our grandmother, but nothing happens. Exhausted and exasperated, we finally give up.

In the early morning hours when I can't sleep, even after another cup of Ruby's specialty tea, I look through Eunice's old books. One is a grimoire. I scan for a sleeping spell or anything that might rid me of thoughts about Janice. My search for that is a waste of time, but I do find a few interesting charms for the shop and its products.

My attention keeps returning to a truth spell. Rereading the ingredients and notes handwritten in the margins by my grandmother about the results, I get lost for another hour. Normally, my sisters and I use magick to help the living, but recalling Robyn's request for assistance, I may have to use a bit to help the dead.

By the time the sun rises, sending a hazy yellow glow through the front windows of the shop, I have no doubt I'll be able to figure this out with or without magick.

It's my morning to run the shop, and I wait for the call to come from Finn, telling us the dinner is canceled, the ball postponed.

It doesn't.

While I suspect Robyn is at the mansion interviewing those who were in attendance when Janice died, I consider ways to get close to Finn and Tiffany.

Did anyone know the biographer's habits, routines? Would they know if she was experimenting with an odd supplement, like so many do these days? Did any of them realize that she was on blood pressure medication?

Three different ones, Robyn said. Janice must have had severe hypertension and anxiety.

I would too if people wanted to kill me.

Dozens of questions roll through my brain. I find myself struggling to focus on the job at hand.

Eventually, the busyness of the day suppresses my endless questions, and when they arise during lulls between customers, I pull out a notepad and sketch out the renovation design. Working with my hands eases my anxiety and calms me.

After dinner, we're sharing a delicious bread pudding for desert, and Uncle Odin asks me to tell him what happened at the mansion. I pull out my sketchbook again, and as I describe my time from the moment I arrived until Finn walked me out, I make a list and outline exactly who was where when the different things happened.

As I'm describing the atrium and Tiffany going on about the prized orchid, Uncle Odin stops me. "Did she tell you what kind it was?"

"She said it was a Tiffany Blue, why?"

He sips decaf coffee, his wizened eyes staring at a spot on the table. One of them is full of cataracts causing blindness in it. Oftentimes, he wears a patch, but not tonight. "I've always loved orchids," he says to no one in particular. "One of the few plants I find most anyone can grow, even if they don't have a green thumb. I've never heard of this Tiffany Blue. Could it be poisonous?"

Uncle Odin often goes off on tangents when we're in the middle of a serious discussion, but this time, I feel a rush of knowing—the plants in the atrium. Could one of them be the source of the unusual toxic compound? "You could be onto something, Uncle Odin."

Most of the time, his comments don't necessarily mean anything, but I make a note on my pad about the flower. "I'll see if I can find out more about it, thank you."

His eyes lift to mine and he smiles. "That would be lovely, my dear."

Having everything written out in front of me soothes my brain enough that I sleep finally, my plan on how to help Robyn taking shape.

NINE

The day of the dinner party arrives, and we close the shop an hour early in order to get ready. We've combed through more of our grandmother's hidden library, but Ruby's had no luck connecting with her spirit. She's determined, however, and regardless, we're all enjoying going through the journals, books, and recipes.

Janice has not reappeared. No word on the poison has come yet, either. I haven't had time to research the orchid.

What if the flower was mixed with the heart medication and caused a deadly reaction?

Ruby discovered a candy recipe book in grandma's stash. Like with her soaps, there's an extra magickal ingredient or two added to the various truffles, mints, and nougats.

Today, Ruby experimented, and while we're

getting dressed for the dinner party, she passes around a plate with samples.

The hard candies are my favorites, especially the lemon drops. There's a tiny hint of lime and lavender in them. I suck on one after another, my nerves over the party and seeing Finn, getting to me.

Zelle insists on doing my hair, taking the dirty blonde locks and curling the ends into soft, lazy ringlets. She doesn't like the outfit I've chosen and insists on dressing me in one of her more daring sapphire blue outfits.

Yikes. My reflection in the full-length mirror is striking, but I'm totally uncomfortable with the plunging neckline, my cleavage on full display. Belle adds a sapphire drop necklace around my neck, and I have to admit the effect is enchanting.

The one positive I find about the dress is it has deep pockets in the folds of the skirt. In one, I tuck lip gloss and cellphone, and in the other, my van keys and license.

Shoes are another issue. With my big feet, I stick to casual tennis shoes, and only have two pair of what would be considered dressy. Neither looks good with the fancy sapphire number, and Zelle digs out pairs of heels from her collection that make me cringe.

They'd all look good with it, but I settle on the pair with the lowest heels, afraid I might trip over myself or break an ankle. I use magick to adjust the size, but they're still a bit tight.

Once we're ready, excitement high, and far too

much sugar in our veins thanks to Ruby's candy, we gather the gift bags and prepare to walk out the door.

My phone buzzes. I start to ignore it, but Belle claims she has to run and pee, so while we wait for her, I glance at it to see an email waiting for me.

"Oh curses," I moan under my breath.

"What?" Zelle swipes bright pink lipstick on her lips.

"It's Jason again. He's still trying to get me to go to the ball with him."

"Tell him you already have a date," Zelle says.

"I'm not going, and how did he get invited, anyway?"

Ruby adjusts one of her earrings. "He's part of the stage crew. You have a standing invitation from Finn, so tell Jason you already have a date."

"What would help is if you guys would once and for all take my profile off that dating app. I have no intention of going out with Jason or anyone else."

Ruby slides on her red cape, tying it around her neck, "Tell you what, sis. You accept Finn's invite, and I'll take it down right now."

"It wasn't really *Finn's* invitation, you know; it was from his mom."

Belle returns and Zelle takes my shoulder, guiding me to the back door. "Good enough. Say you're going, and we'll never bother you about dating again."

As we exit and traipse down the porch steps, I realize I'm outnumbered. It wouldn't be a date, technically, and if I can survive this dinner, then I can survive the theater performance and the ball. Right? "Fine. Do it."

Belle glances between our other two sisters, having missed the gist of the conversation. Her twin winks at her as she pulls out her phone and starts tapping away. "We've convinced Cinder to go to the ball with Finn."

I stick the bags in the back of the van and slam the door. "I'm not going *with* Finn. I am going because his mother asked me."

"But you *are* going." Ruby argues.

As we're about to pull from the parking lot, Matilda suddenly materializes in the back seat. "I can't believe you guys were leaving without me."

Up front, Ruby and I exchange a look. Telling her she can't come could start an ugly fight and we'd all end up turtles or buzzards. "Sorry," I say. "We thought you were busy."

As she pouts, and Belle and Zelle talk about how amazing it will be for me to go to the ball, I bite my tongue.

Ruby gives my arm a squeeze, attempting to reassure me everything will turn out all right.

My greatest fear, even more than Matilda reducing the mansion to ash or some other horrible faux pas, is that Janice's killer may be dining with us tonight.

CHAPTER

TEN

I love my sisters, I do, but there are times I'd like to strangle them.

They tease me incessantly about Finn on the drive to the mansion, chattering non-stop about Tiffany and her fame as well.

I confess that Robyn asked me to stick close to the Starling family to see if I can uncover anything that might tell us what really happened to Janice.

Ruby jokes about me being an undercover agent, and Matilda keeps humming a 70s sitcom theme song connected to a spy show. I've heard the music before, even though I've never seen the show, and I glare at her in the rearview mirror. She winks and continues humming.

When we arrive at the mansion, my sisters *oooh* and *aaah*, exclaiming about the beauty of it. Ruby points out the majestic oaks, dripping with moss, and a series of willows on the south side. Night is just beginning to fall and the lights lining the sweeping drive come to life as we pull in. The water fountain bubbles in a kaleidoscope of colors from hidden LED lights. Multiple cars are parked near the entrance, the occupants already inside.

The wide veranda has been transformed since my earlier visit with dozens of pumpkins, gourds, and urns overflowing with colorful mums, trailing ivy, and ferns. Leaf garlands wind around the railings and giant pillars. Gathered cornstalks and hay bales make inviting displays in the corners. Large rocking chairs are draped with soft throws, and, wound through all of it are hundreds of tiny fairy lights.

Beckoning. Inviting. The elegance is formal, yet cozy and homey. My pulse skips; I feel as though we're about to enter an enchanted castle.

Carrying the box of gift bags up the front steps, my sisters and Matilda trail behind me, continuing to comment about the decor. Ruby rings the doorbell and says under her breath, "Man, if this is any indication, I can't wait to see what the ballroom looks like."

I probably should ask Finn or Ms. Starling if I can bring my sisters to the ball. I'd love to have them there to offset my social awkwardness, and they could help me search for clues. I'm not usually one to invite myself—or them—to an event, but my determination to figure out what happened to Janice supersedes my feelings.

Turning to them and Matilda, I whisper, "Everybody move close together and stand still."

"What are you doing?" Zelle asks as I raise my hand.

I murmur a charm, waving magick over them. "Making sure you're immune to all poisons," I tell her quietly as the front door opens.

I expect Rowena, but it's Finn. He's dressed in a striking gray suit and bright cerulean blue tie that nearly matches his eyes. As dashing as ever, especially when a smile broadens his face, he throws out his hands. "You made it." He lifts the box from my arms and takes in the low-cut dress. "You look stunning."

No one moves, and I'm locked in his gaze for a long moment. I wonder what color his socks are, what it would be like to dance in his arms.

Matilda clears her throat and brushes past me. "You must be Finn. Hope you have room for one more —I'm Matilda, the girls' godmother. I invited myself since I wanted to be sure they're all safe here after what happened."

With some reluctance, he tears his gaze from mine. "Yes, ma'am. Completely understandable. It's nice to meet you. Come on in."

We enter and Rowena rushes forward to help with our jackets. She disappears with them as Finn sets the box on an entryway table and checks me over from head to toe. "You look stunning, Cinder."

"You already said that," I remind him, warmth rising up my neck.

"It bears repeating."

I'm sure Zelle's dress will melt on me, I'm so hot. "You clean up well too."

He takes my hand and pulls it into the crook of his elbow. To my sisters, he says, "Dinner starts in fifteen minutes. Can I get you something to drink?"

We venture into the sitting room and make small talk with the group gathered there. The cast for the play, along with Jamison and Lucinda Dickens, two literary authors who run the theater and fund most of the plays, chat and gossip in small groups. The Dickens write under a pen name and have done screenplays, specializing in murder mysteries.

Finn introduces us to a tall, broad man leaning an elbow on the fireplace mantle and looking uncomfortable. Leo Kingsley is an eccentric millionaire who lives one house over and deals in antiquities and books.

Another supporter of the theater, he has a reserved seat in the balcony. Scuttlebutt around town is that he always sits alone and is about as anti-social as you can get. In our small town, that makes him the focal point of a lot of speculation.

He doesn't offer to shake my hand, but I see his eyes light when they fall on Belle. I introduce her and the other two, and he does offer his hand to her.

A shy smile creeps over her face and she dips her head slightly. "Lovely to meet you, Mr. Kingsley."

Ruby and I exchange a look behind her back. Matilda asks Finn, "About that drink..."

There's a gathering of three women across the

room, heads together and eyes on Finn. All three act in the theater, and one is a former fashion model.

They send me pointed glares at the way Finn has me tucked in close to him, and I give them my most charming smile, loving how it irritates them even more. He releases me to satisfy Matilda's desire for liquor, but once the glass of wine is delivered, he again takes my hand.

The doorbell rings and the middle-aged director of the theater enters moments later. Don Louis Carlos rushes around the room greeting everyone and shaking hands. He's rather short and has a lot of salt in his dark hair, but he's as vibrant and melodramatic as you would expect.

A bell sounds from deep within in the house, and Elsa appears in the doorway to announce dinner is ready. Finn leads the ensemble halfway across the mansion into the east wing and formal dining room.

Multiple chandeliers illuminate a long cherry wood table, crystal water goblets and wine glasses at each place twinkling under the lights. A giant fireplace anchors one end of the room, and a swinging door on the right admits access from the kitchen. Elsa pushes a large cart filled with appetizers into the room as we all find our seats.

Tiffany stands at the head of the table in a white shimmering dress, adorned with tiny gold beads at the cuffs of the sleeves and neckline. Her hair is swept to one side with gold combs. Diamonds drip from her ears, wrap her wrists, and multiple cocktail rings adorn her fingers. She welcomes us and directs the seating arrangement, separating me from my sisters and Finn.

At least he's across from me, his eyes never leaving mine for long as each course is served, and the conversation winds in many directions. The obvious subjects are covered fairly quickly, then Tiffany goes on and on about the silent auction fundraiser.

Don Louis discusses opening night, the Dickens offering what appears to be unsolicited advice about several scenes. Lucinda assures Tiffany they plan to dedicate and rename the theater in her honor.

The aging actress plays her part well throughout dinner, steering conversation away from anything having to do with her biography or the poor woman's death. She puts away as much wine as Matilda, and I notice Callie keeping an eagle eye on her.

At one point, I sneak in a question. "Have you all seen the rare orchid Ms. Starling has?" I turn to her without waiting for anyone's response. "Is the Tiffany Blue difficult to keep alive? Does it require special potting soil or care?"

Our host pauses for a second, eyes narrowing. "All my plants receive expert care. They're like my babies."

"My uncle has a great interest in orchids," I tell her. "I mentioned it to him, and he was curious about it. I was hoping I might visit the atrium tonight and get a picture of it."

This seems to make her happy. "Why, of course. I love to show off my favorite flower."

"I'll take you to see it," Finn offers.

His mother narrows her eyes at me, even though she speaks to Finn. "Thank you, dear."

His interest in me seems to be bothering her now. I bite my lower lip, wondering if she's deemed me unworthy of his attention.

By the time the third course is served, my stomach is busting at the seams. Tiffany is telling a story about something that happened on the set of *The Glass Slippers* and everyone pays rapt attention. Elsa and Rowena come and go as expected, neither of them seeming out of sorts at all. I try to think of a way to talk to each privately, but I'm not sure tonight will offer me that opportunity.

Bonnie Johnson, one of the women who's had her eye on Finn, is sitting on my right. As I sip the last of a good merlot, he's smiling at me, and she accidentally —or *not* so accidentally—knocks an elbow into mine.

I nearly lose my grip on the glass, liquid sloshing over the rim and spilling several large drops onto my dress.

"Oh dear," Bonnie says. Apparently, she's playing the role of Tiffany's character, Katie, in the theater production tomorrow night. "Clumsy me. I'm so sorry."

I grab my napkin and dab at the stains, Ruby catching my eye from across the table and frowning. Matilda clears her throat, and I give both a *down boy* face. Bonnie better be careful, or one of them will turn her dessert into a snake.

"It's okay," I say more to Ruby and our godmother than to the actress. "Is there somewhere I can wash this out?"

Callie, seated four chairs down, leans forward and says, "Use club soda. It always works on wine stains."

Finn gets to his feet, tossing his napkin on his plate. "There's plenty of club soda in the ballroom. I'll take you."

As we exit, I make sure to give Bonnie a big smile. She returns it but it's more of a jeer.

She better be careful, or *I'll* turn her dessert into a snake.

Even though I had a tour with Tiffany the other day, I'd be lost in the mansion if it wasn't for Finn. The ballroom is deeper in this wing, where Tiffany and I didn't go, and I know my sisters would love to see how beautifully decorated it is in anticipation for the upcoming party.

"The bar's nearly stocked," Finn tells me as he leads me past a long table with a white tablecloth displaying an assortment of memorabilia that Tiffany is auctioning off. Most of it means little to me, since I haven't seen the movie, but I expect she'll be able to raise a good amount for the theater.

From behind the bar, Finn pulls out a liter of club soda but looks around with a frown on his face. "No towels. I'll be right back."

He leaves and I stroll around admiring the decorations and wondering what it's like to attend a ball. The last dance I went to was my high school prom, and I sort of hope to never repeat that experience again.

A white placard embossed in gold, designates a place on the table reserved for Tiffany's glass slippers. I'm surprised she would auction them off, but then again, I barely know the woman. I wonder if the rumors about the curse, and Janice dying in them, will make them more valuable or less. Maybe Robyn won't give them back in time, and the point will be moot.

The door opens, but instead of Finn, it's Elsa. Accompanying her is a man carrying a box of liquor bottles that clank as he crosses the open dance floor. Elsa barely glances at me, in the middle of an explanation to him about where to put them and about what time he's to be there to set things up before the ball begins.

She watches the bartender unpack and arrange the bottles behind the bar, arms crossed over her chest. I get the feeling she's inventoried every bottle and will be keeping her eye on him during the ball to make sure all the liquor is accounted for.

I edge closer to her and comment on the decorations, hoping I can delve into more serious questions once we start talking. She continues to watch the man, even as she answers. "If you ask me, the ball should be called off. She's only doing this for the publicity."

"Why?"

"Everything that woman does is for publicity."

"I thought she might cancel since the news about

the poisoning was revealed," I say. "Do you think it's possible Janice ingested the substance accidentally?"

She frowns at me. "How would I know? She was constantly demanding special food, special water—like our water wasn't good enough for her. She even got into it with Rowena. Everyone loves that girl, but not Janice Dubois."

Elsa doesn't appear to love her. "They had an argument?"

"Something to do with the way the girl was washing and ironing her clothes. Plus, she had me washing out that stainless steel travel mug she carried three times a day. She had a thing about germs. She was harder to get along with than Ms. Starling."

"Did you know she had a bad heart? That she was taking medicine for it? Maybe that's why she worried about germs."

Elsa turns her beady eyes on me. "The only thing I knew about her was that she was a spoiled, condescending, entitled witch."

The term raises my hackles, but that may be exactly why she used it. I pretend not to take offense and wonder if Elsa knows I'm a witch, or if she only used the term in place of something worse.

"All I want is to get through the next few days and get things back to normal," she says gruffly.

She snaps her fingers at the man, who looks everything over one more time then follows her out. Finn returns with the towels and helps me with the club soda.

His hand is warm as I take the towel and go rub at a spot. "This isn't even my dress," I explain. "It's Zelle's."

"It must be nice having siblings."

I could magick the stains away, but I enjoy having him to myself, so I keep working with the towel. "I can't imagine life without them."

Finn studies me closely. "Is Cinder short for something else? Cinderella, perhaps?"

The grin in his voice brings my gaze up. "My mom loved fairytales. She named me Cinder, middle name Ella, so yes, it is, in fact."

I know what's coming next, so I nip that in the bud. "Our parents died when I was barely eighteen. You're lucky to still have yours, even if your father isn't around."

"I'm sorry," he says. "And you're right—I *am* lucky to have both of mine."

There's a question that's been in the back of my mind since my tour of the mansion. "So, you live in Atlanta?"

He gently takes the towel and wets a new corner of it with soda. "Worried I live with my mother?"

I blush, accepting the towel and resuming my ministrations. "I'd still live with my parents if they were alive. Our house isn't as huge as your mansion, but it has plenty of space for all of us, and since we work downstairs, there's no reason to move. Your mom mentioned you don't reside here."

He kicks back, leaning on the bar. "I knew the

move from L.A. was going to be hard on her, and I had plenty of stored vacation, so I took time off to ease the transition and make sure she was okay."

I start on the second spot. "What do you think about Janice being poisoned?"

He sighs and glances at the table of memorabilia. "She only arrived last weekend, but she was difficult to get along with. Still, it had to have been an accident."

"What about your mom's shoes?" I'm wondering what he thinks about the curse. "Did you ever figure out why Janice was wearing them?"

He returns to the pile of towels and grabs a fresh one, splashing club soda on it. "There are dozens, if not hundreds of women, who would love to try those shoes on." He shrugs, exchanging towels with me. "Do I think they're cursed? No. On the other hand, there have definitely been a few odd things that have happened to my mother in her career, and in her personal life. Could it be bad luck? Who knows."

"I don't believe in luck, good or bad. I believe we make our own fate, choose our own destiny."

Elbow on the bar top, he studies me again. "You're wise for your age."

"I had to grow up fast in order to keep custody of my sisters, but I also had wise guidance from my godmother and uncle. They dropped their lives to move in and care for us, and we were lucky to have grandparents nearby."

"Your godmother is interesting," he says. "Why didn't you bring your uncle too?"

I give up on the stains, planning to get the rest out later. Tossing the towel on the bar I give him an apologetic look. "Sorry about that. I know you weren't expecting Matilda, but she's an expert at worming her way into things, and she really wanted to see the mansion and meet your mom. She's a big fan."

He shrugs. "I'm used to that."

"You seem to have quite a fan club of your own tonight."

He grins and leans in. "And you, Cinder? Are you in that fan club?"

"Maybe," I say a little flippantly, and give him a return grin. "As long as we're on the subject of me inviting people into your life, would it be possible to score invites for my sisters?"

His eyes dance, barely an inch of space between our faces. "For Cinder Ella? Anything...on one condition."

My heart skips a beat and my question comes out breathy, "What?"

He whispers his request in my ear, sending chills down my spine.

CHAPTER

ELEVEN

The rest of the dinner proceeds with a selection of delicious deserts, and I have to admit Elsa is an amazing cook, even if she is grumpy.

Every time Finn glances at me, I have to fight a blush. Nothing escapes my sisters, and as the group exits the dining room to get their gift bags, they all try to pull me aside and ask questions. Matilda simply watches me with a knowing expression. Unfortunately, I don't make it to the atrium to get pictures of the orchid.

The bargain I struck with Finn involves a trade—ball invitations in exchange for the favor of walking me home.

After passing out the gift bags, I let my sisters know I won't be chauffeuring them home. Matilda takes the keys and they give me wicked grins as they say goodnight to Ms. Starling and leave.

The air is crisp and cool as we walk away from Millionaires Row toward downtown. I'm cursing Zelle's shoes, as my feet are killing me, but the pain is simply background noise because I'm happily focused on Finn and the beautiful night sky.

I also have a job to do, so after enjoying a brief comfortable silence, I bring up Elsa. "Has the chef been with your mom long?"

Holding my hand, he shoots me a look from the corner of his eye. "A while, why?"

"She's an amazing cook. I haven't eaten that well in years."

Ruby's good and she makes a lot of meals, but I long for the days when our mom would get in the kitchen and create the most delicious master-pieces. I'm sure she used magick to help, but I've never been able to replicate any of her recipes. She never followed any or wrote her versions down. "I can barely boil water and not burn toast," I admit. "I'm in awe of anyone who can cook even mildly well."

His fingers tighten on mine. "I can handle the basics, and Mother can actually do pretty darn well. She just chooses to have a chef on staff."

"Did you know anything about an argument between Rowena and Janice? I think it had to do with Janice's clothes or something."

Our stroll comes to a stop and he turns to me. "Never heard about it. Did Rowena tell you that?"

I shake my head. "Elsa mentioned it tonight in the

ballroom. We were discussing the fact your mom decided to still have the auction and dance."

He looks uncomfortable, and I want to kick myself when he releases my hand. "Staff problems are always an issue. Elsa wasn't happy when Mother moved here, and she's a bit bossy, if you haven't noticed. Rowena was also upset about the relocation. I can't tell you how many maids, cooks, and gardeners my mom has gone through over the years."

That brings up another person I haven't investigated. "The gardener, what was his name?"

I can tell Finn is beginning to wonder what I'm up to. "Jackson."

Right. I'd forgotten. "So he takes care of the atrium, as well as the gardens and yard?"

"Why all the questions?"

Yep he's onto me. I give him a smile and tell him the truth. "I was there that day, and the whole thing upsets me. Who knows where Janice got the poison? I worried about bringing my sisters to dinner tonight, to be honest. I'm trying to come to grips with all of this."

He runs a hand through his hair. "You're right. I'd be protective of my family too, and I am, but whatever happened had to be accidental. No one else has become sick, so I don't know what she picked up or how, but everyone at dinner was safe."

I decide to quit probing, hoping Finn will relax his guard again. I resume walking, and glance back at him. "I really appreciate the invitations for my sisters."

He joins me, but he doesn't reach for my hand.

"You guys should attend the theater performance as well. Our treat."

It might save me from watching the movie, so I consider it. "I'm a fan of the theater. I'd love to."

His fingers brush mine, gentle and teasing. "I might actually enjoy it then."

"What do you mean?"

"Do you know how many times I've had to watch that movie? My mom is stuck in a time warp, her best memories involving the film and those crazy shoes. I seriously thinking if I had to watch it one more time, I might jab my eyes out. I love her, but I can quote every line in my sleep."

The comfortable silence between us returns, and I'm happy to simply walk next to him, his fingers skimming mine as the stars twinkle overhead.

My family obviously beat us home, but the shop is dark, a single light left on for me. Finn sees me to the shop door, and I pull out my key. "Would you like to come in?"

"I should get back and help Elsa and Rowena straighten up."

That he's willing to do that causes a warm sensation in my chest. "Do you think the rest of the guests have left by now?"

He cants his head. "There are always a few who linger. I can probably spare a minute or two."

"Avoiding your fan club?" I tease.

"Absolutely."

I let us in, the soft glow of the workroom light illuminating enough of the shop that we can make our way through it without running into the displays. The mansion was incredible, but I love the smell of my home, and feel the tenseness in my bones from social-izing, release.

Finn looks around at the changes I've already made and points at the fireplace. "Did I miss it the other day?"

"It was hidden by shelving. Once I clean it up, it will add cool ambience to the display floor." I explain that I've sketched preliminary plans for what I want to do with the rest of the layout once I have the time and the money.

"You've drawn out your ideas?"

I can see the architect in him is interested, and I backpedal. "Rough ones. Very rough. I'm no architect and don't have your talent. I do know that wall,"—I indicate the north side—"is load-bearing, so I can't take it out. I can still expand the opening here though." Another point.

He nods and starts talking about support beams and other things. He offers options I hadn't realized might work. "I'd love to see your sketches," he says.

I'm feeling warm and happy, so surprisingly, I agree to show them to him. "Follow me."

I lead him upstairs to the kitchen where I left my book earlier, hastily flipping pages to show him the storeroom, workroom, and expanded showroom. No point in him seeing my notes about the day Janice died.

Along with my book is a plate of candies from Ruby. She's left a note asking us to try them.

My sister. I'm not the only psychic in the family. If only my sight could tell me the truth about Janice's death.

I mention the secret room and Ruby's new fascination with making candy from our grandmother's recipes we discovered. Finn brightens at this and is more than happy to taste test. "A secret room? In the turret? I can't wait to see that."

I still feel like I'm about to burst from Elsa's meal, but I sneak one of the caramels and enjoy the richness as it melts on my tongue. "It's amazing. I'll take you up there when I get the lights working."

Finn nods with excitement, and chooses a dark chocolate. "These are delicious. Mother would love them. Do you think your sister would make more and bring them up to the house?"

Some days I don't know how Ruby does everything she does, and now she's making candies from scratch. "I'm sure she could. She told me yesterday that our grandfather, who lives on the other side of the woods, loved the ones she took him. He's really not supposed to have all that sugar, so she's experimenting with using natural sweeteners, but I know she has an order from him to make a whole bunch."

For the next hour, he devours the candy and I explain my sketches. Luckily, Finn doesn't make fun of my amateurish drawings, and is able to lend ideas to help me. What I wish to do within the confines of the structure is a big undertaking.

Several times during the course of our discussion, our hands brush, and our teasing escalates. He has a sharp wit, and I'm just plain sassy, so it feels good to find someone like him who dishes out as much as I do.

"Can you recommend a soap for me?" he asks. "I'd like to try one of your lines."

Returning to the shop, I flick on lights. Our men's line has been growing, and I'm proud to show it off. I have him close his eyes as I wave different varieties under his nose. "Tell me which smell you like best."

He picks a lemongrass that's part of our charcoal line. When he opens his eyes, I show it to him. "This is good for cleaning, but if you're sensitive it can strip the natural oil from your skin, so I recommend following it up with our goat's milk lotion."

I reach for a sample bottle. "Anytime you exfoliate or shave, this will restore the pH balance to your skin."

He looks over the shelf containing more of the products in that line up. "I'll take one of everything."

"Are you sure?"

He nods. "I want to try it all."

I point to a bottle on the shelf. "This is a serum for your beard. Are you hiding one of those somewhere?"

He laughs. "I'll give it to Jackson and let him try it."

"Okay. Let me get a bag."

He insists on paying, even though I feel weird about it. "Consider it helping with the expansion," he says.

That I can do. At the door, bag weighted down from all of the products, he takes my hand and kisses my knuckles. "Please tell me you'll come to the ball."

How can I say no?

"I'll come...on one condition."

The tit for tat makes him laugh. "And what would that be?"

"I want to be clear it's not a date."

His face falls a little, but then I see the challenge rising in his eyes. "What do you have against dating?"

Oh, just everything. "I don't know exactly what's going on between us, and I totally appreciate every-thing you've done for me this week. I like you a lot, Finn, but the thing is, I have responsibilities. Big ones. A romantic relationship is..."

I hesitate to say what's on my tongue. It sounds lame when I'm standing here in a shaft of moonlight looking at my very own Prince Charming.

Finn kisses my knuckles again. "I'm not giving up. Those responsibilities? Maybe you should let someone help you with them."

But he won't be here forever, and even if he's only a few hours away, a long-distance relationship would add more problems to my cauldron already full of them.

Besides the fact, he doesn't know I'm a witch. I can't wait to throw that in the middle of our current friendship, or whatever this is. "Look, there's things about me you don't know."

He touches the end of my nose with his. "And I

can't wait to find all of them out. I know this is happening fast, but I've never felt this way about anyone before."

I haven't either and it scares me.

Planting a light kiss on my cheek, he reaches for the doorknob. "See you tomorrow."

He leaves me standing there, feeling slightly dazed.

Later, I curl up with McAlister, and tell him about the evening as he plays with an old sock of mine. I review everything I learned.

Then I call Robyn to tell her about Rowena and the argument with Janice. She assures me she'll look into it. She hints that even Tiffany could be a suspect, and my heart falls.

"Tiffany? Why would she kill her own biographer?"

"You just told me Elsa claimed she'd do anything for publicity. None of us know this woman, and if she wanted publicity for her book? The death of her biographer in the middle of all of this would certainly bring her a lot. It already has."

True. Belle's been keeping up on the internet explosion and everything that's happened with Tiffany. It appears our aging star is back in the Hollywood limelight.

"What do you think about her son?" Robyn asks out of the blue.

I find myself blushing again. Good grief. When was the last time any guy made me feel like this? "He's... incredible. Down to earth, well mannered."

There's a pregnant pause before she says, "If anything happens with Tiffany, he stands to inherit her estate."

There's a heaviness to her statement, things unsaid that I'm supposed to divine. "What are you saying?"

"Is it possible Finn set his mother up as a murderer?"

I leap off the bed, startling McAlister, who curls up, becoming a pin cushion. "That's ridiculous! He loves her, and he's very protective of her. The only reason he's here is to help her with the move and getting everything established."

A heavy sigh. "If Dubois was purposely poisoned, every single person at the mansion is a suspect at this point."

When we hang up, the joy and lightness I felt during the evening turns into a sour pit in my stomach.

TWELVE

atilda and I are running the shop the next day when Robyn visits. She looks tired and I leave Matilda to the cash register while I take her to the kitchen and make her a cup of chai tea.

She removes her jacket, the SCPD badge on her belt gleaming in the light before she sits down. She rubs both hands over her face. "I re-questioned the maid and her story is off about where she was when Janice died. The lab hasn't gotten back to us, but I went through that greenhouse. There are a lot of exotic plants, and I wouldn't be surprised if one of them is our culprit."

"There's a special orchid that Tiffany is wild about. I wanted to get a picture of it last night, but didn't. Uncle Odin mentioned it might be poisonous, but I haven't had a chance to research it. It's called Tiffany Blue."

Robyn scribbles down the name in her tiny notebook. "Named after her?"

"I don't think so, but I assume that's a big reason why she's enamored with it."

"We searched the maid's apartment on the estate and found nothing. We took her phone and laptop, and the IT group is looking into any searches she did, or anything else that might point to her being our killer."

I join her at the table with my own tea. "If the poisoning *wasn't* accidental," I add.

She gives me a tired look. "Yes, of course. There is a slight chance it was."

"Janice may have been messing around with one of the plants, not realizing it was poisonous," I offer. I've thought a lot about this, examined multiple theories. "Maybe one of them had berries and she ate it, not knowing what it would do to her. Or she picked a pretty flower, or rubbed a leaf, and then put her fingers in her mouth. She could've thought something was a harmless herb and stuck a piece in her stainless steel mug."

I'm grasping at straws, and Robyn nods as if she's already considered all of these options. "I'll admit, I've seen pretty weird things in my time on the force, and it's all possible, but not probable. We already checked the mug. No dice. We don't know if it's fast-acting, or something she may have ingested days beforehand."

We sit in silence for a long moment.

"The one thing about the maid that bugs me,"

Robyn goes on, "is that her fingerprints were on the shoes."

We stare at each other and I fiddle with the end of my sketchbook still lying here from last night. "She may have moved them at some point to clean, or brought them to Ms. Starling, or was checking to see how much space they needed on the auction table."

"Or she put them on Janice's feet after she was dead. We also found her fingerprints on the biographer's shoes. She claims she was constantly having to pick them up and move them and that's why."

That's an angle I hadn't considered. "If Rowena was the killer, why would she trade the shoes and put the famous ones on Janice?"

"You've heard the rumors, right? There are all kinds of people who believe those shoes are bad luck. Maybe she thought it would create a diversion. That we'd think the curse killed the woman."

There's plenty who would buy that. "Surely, she'd know you'd look beyond that and discover Janice had been poisoned."

Robyn shrugs, finishes her tea, and rises to grab her jacket off the back of the chair. "Small town police are usually considered imbeciles." Her phone rings and she gives me a look to excuse the interruption before she answers. "Detective Wood."

During a pause, I rise to wash her cup and put it in the sink. As I return, she meets my eyes. "Got it. Yes, sir, I'll go up there right now and bring her in."

She disconnects and pockets the phone. "They

found documents on the maid's computer about poisonous plants. Some other stuff as well that I'm not at liberty to tell you."

"Oh no," I say. "You think she did it?"

Robyn pats my shoulder as she's leaving. "Good work, Cinder. Thanks for your help. I'll let you know what happens."

I think about contacting Finn and checking on him and his mom, but we're busy and I can't for a while. Belle relieves Matilda at three, and Zelle comes in shortly afterwards. "We're going shopping," she announces.

"You couldn't get the stains out of the dress?" I ask. "Even with magick?"

"I took it to the cleaners and it'll be fine. That's not why we're going shopping. You need a dress for the ball."

More like *she* wants one. "Don't you have something I can wear?"

"What fun is that? I already covered you for the dinner, now you have the play and the ball. You need new clothes and shoes."

Ruby, who's in the kitchen making candy, comes out and insists I go. "It'll do you good."

"I need to call Finn," I declare.

Zelle grabs my arm and tugs me to the door. "Finn's fine. Text him later."

My sister and I spend the next hour and a half at dress boutiques. Story Cove has kept big box stores out, and there's no shopping mall, so the small stores flourish.

Mrs. Grimmly, owner of Red Apple Apparel nearly falls over when she sees Zelle dragging me into her dress shop. "Why Cinder," she says in her soft southern voice. "I haven't seen you since the Matilda incident."

Another memory I'd rather avoid, involving wonky magick and a rack of bras that exploded. "I'm still so sorry for that."

A gracious smile that lacks true warmth appears. "How I can help you today?"

"She needs something for the ball," Zelle tells her, already looking at a forest green number on a mannequin.

"Oh, marvelous," the owner says, eyes lighting up. No doubt because of the dollar signs she sees. I'm definitely paying for those ruined bras, one way or another.

If hell were a place filled with satin, silk, taffeta, and pearls, Mrs. Grimmly's shop would be it. I grit my teeth, and try not to look as self-conscious as I feel when she and Zelle parade a dozen different options past me.

They all make me itch. I'm so uncomfortable every time I slip one of them on and look at myself in the mirror, my hopes at finding something beautiful—as well as functional—dwindle by the minute.

One of them does cause my eyes to glaze over. A stunning gold, drop-waisted, sparkling satin makes all the others pale in comparison. I'm mesmerized by it, even after I see the price tag and nearly faint. I desperately want to try it on, but I can't breathe when I think about how much it costs.

Frustrated after an hour, Zelle decides to switch gears. "How about we start with shoes. Sometimes you discover the perfect pair of heels first, then find something to wear with them. I always say shoes make the woman."

"You have dozens and dozens of fancy pairs in your closet," I counter, seeing the price tags. "I can wear one of those."

She stifles a breath, the air lifting her pink tipped bangs, and gives me a sisterly glare. "Indulge me, just this once. Let me make you over."

Feeling slightly guilty at not enjoying the process, I force a nod. Again, items are paraded in front of my nose, but the one pair I like doesn't come in my size. Others pinch, or make me topple over from the height.

At least they're all new. They tickle my gift, and I see flashes of the places they were manufactured, the way they were boxed, sense them being shipped. The red wedges was tried on by Betsy Donovan while yelling at her kids. Zelle's friend, Laurie, felt great disappointment in the fact she couldn't afford the black strappy sandals.

I know the feeling. With a growing headache, I tell Zelle I'm not going to the ball. There's no dress or shoes here that will work. Defeated, I just want to go home.

My sister's disappointment rides me, but she grabs my hand, thanks Mrs. Grimmly, and takes me back to the house. I don't mention that part of my issue with the whole thing is the cost. Some of those price tags nearly made me faint. What I can do with hundreds of dollars toward our building fund is my priority, not buying a dress I'll wear once and then go to waste in the back of my closet.

Ruby, Belle, and Matilda are also disappointed when we show up empty-handed. Matilda declares that I can't show up at the ball in a flower sack, and I argue that I just might, mostly because I'm feeling as disappointed as they are and it makes me scrappy.

My sisters march me upstairs, leaving our godmother to tend the store, and Zelle raids her closet. She emerges with a simple rose-colored sheath that falls to the floor with a discreet side slit.

When I put it on, I see myself in a whole new light. It's not overly fancy, but very classy, and I imagine one of our grandmothers wearing something like this in the 1920s. Zelle finds a rhinestone belt and wraps it around my waist, and my straight figure takes on curves.

"Now for the shoes," she says, as I'm ogling my reflection.

A pair that match the sheen and color of the dress float out from her closet. I strap them on and get a flash of the last time she wore them—she was dancing, feeling young, free, and lighthearted.

She sees the emotions cross my face. "Oh that."

Her eyes get a faraway look in them. "It was a couple years ago. Remember Randy?"

Belle glances up from her book, Jayne perched in her lap. "The tire guy?"

Randy Rickertsen owns the auto repair store. Zelle dated him for a few months, but he smelled like rubber all the time, and she couldn't stand it. "He took me to that fancy country club upstate. What a great night that was."

Sitting on the edge of her bed, I remove the shoes and look at them. "I'll wear them," I tell her, "if that's alright with you."

She claps her hands together in delight. "The sapphire necklace and earrings you wore to the dinner will go perfect with this as well. I'll do your hair and Matilda can do your make up."

Feeling relieved, I shrug out of the dress and thank her profusely, wondering what Finn will think when he sees me, and liking the idea I can simply go and be myself this time. I don't need to ask leading questions or worry about Janice anymore. I can just be a young woman, wearing pretty clothes, and dancing with a guy she's fallen soap over candlestick for.

CHAPTER

THIRTEEN

Tiffany Starling's arrival in the shop that afternoon surprises all of us. She looks like an aging rock star in rhinestone-studded jeans, a furry vest, huge sunglasses and a lot of leather everywhere else.

As I'm helping a customer complete a purchase, she flies across the showroom and grabs me by the shoulders. "I need you," she says, my customer forced to step back. "The drain in the guest bathroom is plugged. Who knows what one of the guests put down it last night. Finn told me the other day you know how to fix a clogged drain. I need you to come to the house and help me."

I'm so startled all I do is stammer, then excuse myself from the customer and pull Tiffany aside. "Can't you get a plumber?"

"The only one in town is down with the flu and won't get to the mansion until after the ball. Finn had to run to Atlanta on business for my charity—documents that need to go with the auction items to prove their authenticity. There's no one else who can fix it in time. *Please.*"

I glance at Ruby behind the counter and she gives me a finger wave encouraging me to go. I face Ms. Starling again. "I'll be there in a few minutes. Just have to gather my tools."

She throws her arms around me in a flamboyant embrace. "Oh, thank you. I knew I could count on you."

She exits, and shaking my head, I apologize to my customer and help her finish her purchase. Once she's out the door, I double-check with Ruby. "Are you sure you can handle the shop alone? I don't know how long I'll be gone."

"I'll grab Matilda and Uncle Odin if need be. Go ahead."

When I get to the mansion, Callie answers the door, I assume because Rowena is down at the police station. Callie looks surprised. I explain that Ms. Starling wants me to fix the sink in the guest bath.

"What?" Callie doesn't move out of the doorway nor invite me in, her eyebrows squishing down and causing lines on her forehead. "There's nothing wrong with that bathroom."

If there's not I'm going to be aggravated. "She told me the sink is clogged."

Callie leans on the door and taps a foot in impatience. "News to me, but then why would she tell me anything?"

I have no answer to that and suspect it's rhetorical, so keep my mouth shut.

"I'm sorry you had to come all this way, but I'll handle the issue." She turns, ready to shut the door in my face, when Tiffany appears at the top of one of the grand staircases.

"There you are." She hustles down the carpeted steps in her slippers and says to Callie, "I'll show her the bath. You go finish that list I gave you."

Callie has her back to me, but I sense her rolling her eyes. "I just used the bathroom. The sink is fine."

As Tiffany grabs my hand to pull me inside, I remain silent. The woman's anxiety is high, probably because her biographer is dead, her housekeeper arrested, and the theater performance, silent auction, and ball are coming up in short order. All I want to do is fix this sink and get back to Enchanted.

Callie steps in front of us, as if to have a showdown with Tiffany. "I'll pour that toxic drain cleaner in it and that will clear the pipes." She gives me an apologetic glance before saying to Ms. Starling, "Really, Tiff, you're making a big deal over nothing."

Ms. Starling ignores her, raising her chin and tugging me past. "I'm going to have a hundred people here tomorrow night. The drain can't be clogged!"

Callie follows us, arguing half-heartedly, then silently disappears before her friend and boss deposits me in a hallway of dark wood and an expensive wool floor runner. I don't remember this from my tour, but a lot of the previous visit is a blur. The walls are lined with paintings in gilded frames and sconces provide the only light, shadows falling heavily everywhere.

Luckily, inside the bathroom, there's better light, and I'm not surprised that this functional space is as lavishly decorated as the rest of the mansion. As far as powder rooms go, this one's bigger than my entire bedroom, and boasts lush carpet, elaborate wallpaper, and a chandelier.

She leaves, assuring me she has dozens of things to wrap up today, and I'm grateful for her absence. With my tools and bucket in hand, I climb under the vanity and start playing with the pipes.

A few days ago, it was my sister's voice that startled me while working under a sink. Now, in the deathly quiet of the luxurious guest bath, it's a deep *buzzbuzzbuzz* and a soft blue light that make me shoot up and whack my head on the underside of the golden basin above.

"Ouch!" I flop back, rubbing my forehead and swearing. The noise keeps up, sounding like a cell-phone on vibrate, but it's so close to my head, I'm confused. It's not mine and it's coming from above my head and to the left.

In my experience, vanities and sinks don't buzz or glow.

I move my work light to shine it in the direction of the noise. Whatever it is seems to be taped under the middle vanity drawer.

Squeezing down, I flash the beam into the slim crevasse. I'm not sure what I'm looking at, the black rectangular box falling silent. Craning my neck, I see a screen, and the size and shape of the box reminds me of a garage door opener. On the screen is a set of digits that looks like a phone number.

A long time ago, Uncle Odin had one of these—a pager. Why would someone hide a pager in here?

For several long seconds, I simply stare at it, finding no good reason for it to be here. Taking my phone out I snap a photo of the number displayed on the screen. Over the next few minutes, I finish fixing the sink, my fingers itching to dial that number, and see who's on the other end.

If I dial from my phone, the individual won't recognize my number, and may not pick up. But maybe they will. Another idea hits, and I shine my light around under the sink, searching for a hidden cellphone or anything else suspicious.

No luck.

Curiosity may have killed the cat, but it may someday kill me as well. Holding my phone with one hand, I sweep my other over the dial pad releasing a burst of suppression magick to make my number show as unidentified. With a giant inhale to steady my nerves, I dial.

A phone rings four times on the other end, and I'm about to hang up, believing no one's going to answer. Just before I do, there's a click and open air.

I hold my breath. Should I say something or keep silent?

I can't decide and after the long pause, a man's voice startles me when he asks "Is everything still in play for Saturday?"

I'm afraid to respond, more than just making a soft grunt as an affirmation. At that moment, there's a knock on the door and I jump, automatically disconnecting the line. The wooden door cracks open an inch, revealing Finn's face.

"Hey, there. Mother said you were here." He widens the door and I pocket my phone. "Sorry about this. She could have waited until I got back. I would've fixed it."

Pulse racing, I begin gathering tools and sticking them in the bucket. "No problem, easy fix. It's just an old pipe that hasn't been cleaned out in a while. Should be fine now."

He walks me out, carrying the bucket of tools. "How about lunch before you go? I'll prepare my famous turkey sandwich for you."

"Oh no. I really need to get back to the shop."

"It's the least I can do," he insists.

I keep thinking about the pager and the man's voice on the other end. What's Saturday?

The play and the ball?

On the heels of that, I wonder, could this have something to do with Janice's death?

I turn to Finn. "Okay, you're on. Lunch would be great, but let's go out, okay?"

He seems happy I've accepted the invitation. "No problem. I haven't been to many restaurants in town yet. Can you recommend a good one? Not that Rooster place, though, okay?"

Definitely not. But I know a great eatery, and it will give me an opportunity to question him more about his mom and the staff. Dread has settled into my stomach about Rowena and her innocence. "Nothing fancy, but the Enchanted kitchen is always open."

FOURTEEN

I can't boil water, but I make a mean grilled cheese.

Because I'm trying to impress Finn, I throw in a side of tomato soup, straight from the can.

He's good natured about it and claims it's the best soup and sandwich he's ever had. He also mentions how much he digs my brightly colored pumpkin socks.

"Quite a surprise about Rowena," I say when we're halfway through lunch.

He swallows a mouthful of sandwich. "I'm having a hard time with the whole thing, to be honest. Rowena is kind of..."

"What?" I prompt when he doesn't finish.

He wipes his fingers on the napkin. "Well, timid, mousy, if you know what I mean. As far as I can tell, the police have no motive. Why would she kill Janice?"

"Elsa told me they had a big argument."

"I heard about that. They got into it over Janice's

clothes, I guess. Seems extreme to go from that to murder, don't you think?'

I stir my soup in contemplation. "Maybe there's more to it than what we know. What does your mom think?"

"She was in tears this morning. She likes Rowena and the girl fed her ego, so that was a plus. Rowena dreams of being a star and is always asking Mother for pointers."

"I don't think Elsa cared for Janice," I muse.

"Elsa doesn't like anybody."

"And Jackson? He has plenty of access to, and knowledge about plants, right?"

He sips his iced tea and points at me. "That's why you were so interested in him last night."

Busted. "I'm trying to figure out why anyone would want to kill Janice. She did apparently have enemies, including a mafia boss, from a series of unauthorized biographies she wrote, but seeing as she was staying at your mansion and working with your mom, I'm ruling those people out."

He leans in conspiratorially. "Unless Jackson is only posing as a gardener, and he's really the mafia guy."

I snicker. "Is that possible?"

Finn barks a laugh. "He's been with Mother for nearly fifteen years. He knows his plants, but I don't think he gave Ms. Dubois a second glance. I highly doubt he poisoned her."

"Okay, but the more I think about it, he's the one

who has the most access to poisonous plants, even those not in the atrium."

"You really think the poisoning was intentional?"

I really do. "If you had to pick someone to commit murder by poison, who would it be? Elsa or Rowena?"

He thinks about it as if it's a real question, chewing more sandwich. "Elsa. She's the cook. Easy for her to slip something into the food. Or the wine. Janice liked wine."

I think of the stainless steel mug, and also about Matilda and her 'magick potion.' "Robyn had them test the mug Janice used and it came up clean."

"She drank wine from a glass. A very expensive one, I might add."

"If Rowena is as timid as you say, she might also be gullible."

"Meaning?"

I fiddle with my napkin, wiping butter from my fingers. "Easy to set up for murder."

Finn sips his sweet tea. "Maybe I should talk to your cousin, the detective."

"So you agree that it's possible Elsa may be behind this?"

He shrugs. "My gut says Rowena is innocent. I don't know why she was doing internet searches about poisonous plants, but she was in the mansion from dawn to nightfall, leaving her apartment empty and simple to access. If someone is setting her up, maybe I can figure out who."

Robyn will kill me for putting Finn on the case,

since he's still under suspicion. "Don't worry about it. I'll mention it to her. My gut can't come to grips with it being Elsa, either. She's a little abrasive, and doesn't seem to like most of us, but she doesn't strike me as a stealthy killer."

"I feel like we're playing Clue," he says, dipping the last piece of his sandwich into his soup.

"You've played the game?"

"Of course. Haven't you? Great board game. I love it."

This makes me inordinately happy. My folks used to play it with me all the time. It was my favorite game growing up, and Belle was the only sister who would play with me. I think my mom and dad felt pity when I couldn't get more than her interested in a game. At least once a month, they'd insist we all sit down to a game. "Are you any good at it?"

He eyes me like a true competitor. "Maybe. Are you?"

I win every time—and I don't use magick. Still, in case he's a future adversary, it's best to put on my poker face. "Maybe," I echo his reply.

A grin tugs at the corner of his mouth. "I sense a challenge on the table."

"You're perceptive."

Savannah strolls in, flicking the end of her tail and sniffing the air. She rubs against Finn's leg. "Beautiful cat. What's his name?"

She rears back and fixes him with a glare. "Her," I correct. "This is Savannah."

He offers to scratch under her chin and she licks his fingers, probably because they smell like grilled cheese.

After another chin rub, Finn shoves his bowl back. "Say, I know an investor who would be interested in working with you. He'd offer you a loan for the expansion in return for a small percentage of profit. Short term, of course."

My stomach tightens. "Is that so? How short?"

One shoulder shrugs as though it's not a big deal. "Say twenty-four months? That would give you time to get the expansion done and start showing a profit on the new products."

I hate the idea, but I try to keep it off my face. "This investor is someone you know personally?"

"Of course." I wonder if it's him, but why wouldn't he just come out and tell me so? Maybe because he knows I'd turn him down flat? Jeez, I won't even go on a date with him, much less consider him as a business partner.

He eyes me warily, as if sensing my reluctance. "I can set up a meeting if you want to explore the idea."

I toy with my napkin, folding and refolding it. How nice it would be to allow someone to swoop in and solve my problems. Someone with gorgeous blue eyes and plenty of money.

"Let me talk to my sisters before we do that. The shop is as much theirs as it is mine, and while I hope to make the business successful enough that all four of us can work here full-time, it's a joint venture, and they have to be onboard."

"Absolutely," he agrees, getting up to leave. "Is there any more of that candy around?"

There are none in the kitchen, but I've stolen a handful of them and stashed them in my room. I tell him to wait there while I retrieve them. McAlister is awake, so I bring him, too.

When I return to the kitchen, I introduce my hedgehog to Finn. He's completely infatuated with the little guy, asking me a dozen questions about him, and tickling his belly

McAlister, unsure of what's going on snubs his nose at Finn initially, hoping for a piece of candy. Finn laughs, and I do, too.

Then Finn squeezes one of my hands and leaves, his smile taking a piece of my heart with him.

FIFTEEN

Thanks to the dinner party, we receive a big candle order from Lucinda Dickens. Not to be totally outdone by Ms. Starling, she's decided to give each member of the cast one of our specialty crystal candles called Success. It features prosperity essential oils, including cinnamon and frankincense, as well as sparkling citrine crystal chips.

Ruby and I work on them that evening, while Belle cleans up the shop and closes out the register. It was a good day, and I feel my happiness weaving its way into the candles as I melt the wax and add the color chips and good-smelling scents.

Our familiars, along with Savannah, are present, each playing or sleeping. Zelle rushes in, ready to assist after her last appointment at the salon, and Rumpelstiltskin greets her with a high-pitched chatter. She gives him a hug and he joyfully dances around the room after she releases him.

Our energy is light, and I enjoy hanging out with all three of them, as I also sift through my doubts and theories concerning Janice, the shoes, and what I found at Ms. Starling's. Discussing it with my sisters sorts it out in my own head.

Robyn is going to stop by so I can show her the picture I snapped of the pager and explain how I contacted the person on the other end—the man who asked about tomorrow.

Belle hums as she carries the cash drawer past us on her way to the office safe. "Why would anyone use a pager?"

I check the temp on the soy wax and remove the pitcher from the burner. "I keep coming back to that. In this day and age, almost everyone carries a cellphone."

Zelle doesn't respond, and Ruby shrugs a shoulder. "Maybe it was left by the previous owner of the mansion. The bigger question to me, is why was it taped in that particular place?"

Belle stops at the office and turns back. "Some older people are more accustomed to them, come to think of it. They don't like cellphones all that much. Daisy carried one up until a few months ago when her grandson was here and took her cellphone shopping. She really only used the pager for emergencies, and I think it had sentimental value to her since her husband carried it for business until he passed."

"Why hide it under a bathroom sink?" Ruby asks

again as she measures out the amount of scent we need. "I don't get it."

Another question I have no answer for. "What if you committed a crime and you didn't want the pager linked to you? You could easily hide it in the mansion. The box was dirty, like it'd been around a long time, or had something spilled on it. I suppose if you were concerned about someone searching your room, you'd find an innocuous place like the guest bath to stash it in."

Zelle washes up and measures out more wax for the next hand-poured batch. "That mansion is huge. You'd think there'd be a better spot."

"But that room has had multiple people going in and out of it recently," Belle counters, leaning on the doorframe. "If you wanted to keep suspicion off yourself and put it on others, a place like that, where all the guests to the house go, is quite perfect."

We fall silent a moment, processing that idea while we work. It makes sense to me and I begin listing all the possibilities. "In the last several weeks, there have been the movers, decorators, the play cast and director, the donors for the theater, us... I mean, dozens of people have had access to it. Then there's the staff, Finn, and Ms. Starling. That's a lot of folks traipsing through that house, any and all of whom could have used that bathroom."

"What do you think the guy meant about everything still being on for Saturday?" Zelle asks.

"I've been thinking about it all day," I reply. "Whatever it is, I have the feeling it's bad."

"Well, it may have nothing to do with Rowena or Janice's death." Belle pushes off the frame. She is forever looking on the bright side. "It would be nice if we could simply have a fun night at the theater and enjoy the ball afterward. Hopefully, Robyn gets it all straightened out quickly."

"Are you anticipating dancing with a certain millionaire who might be there?" her twin teases.

Belle is very fair and flushes a bright pink. Her lips twitch with a smile. "Leo will be at the play, but I don't plan to see him at the ball. From what I gather, it's not his type of social event."

That makes two of us. I feel an odd connection to the guy. "You never know," I say, trying to think as positively as she usually does. "He might surprise you."

"It would be a delight to see him. Either way I intend to enjoy myself." She disappears into the office.

Ruby begins labeling the glass containers for Ms. Dickens' order. "He might like our Blackbeard products," she calls to Belle. "Why don't you call him and see if he wants you to bring him any?"

Silence, and then she reappears. "He *could* use help with that beard," she muses, more to herself than us. "Maybe I'll take a sample of serum to the play as a gift."

"If he ever wants a trim," Zelle offers, "I'm happy to go to his house if that helps."

Belle smiles, pitching in with the candles. "I'll let him know."

Uncle Odin joins us after we've poured the candles and they're beginning to set. He's wearing his eye patch today and carrying a thick book. *The Encyclopedia of Common Household Plants* is filled with colorful pictures, descriptions, and tips on taking care of them. He opens it to a page he has bookmarked and shows me a picture of a houseplant with large green leaves and a stalky trunk. "Does Ms. Starling have any of these in her greenhouse?"

I study the picture, searching my memory. "Yes? I think so, but they were bigger than that, and I believe they had variegated leaves. Why?"

He uses a wrinkled finger to show me a line about the level of toxicity the plant contains. "This is a common houseplant most people don't realize is poisonous. Let me show you a few more."

"I thought you were interested in her orchid?"

He flips pages and stops at a plant with narrower, glossy leaves and large white flowers shooting up from the center. "I researched them, and out of the thirty-thousand varieties, it appears none are poisonous. Who knew?" He shrugs. "So I begin looking into other plants."

I'm pretty sure I've seen this one. I tap the picture. "There are a bunch of these throughout the house, as well as in the atrium. They're beautiful."

Again, he points to the description where it states this one is moderately poisonous. Zelle and Ruby gather as he files past multiple more. I recognize ivy, and discover it's another common houseplant that surprises me. "She has these in multiple places, including in the front parlor."

"Only mildly poisonous, so it would take a significant amount to harm a healthy person." He turns to another page and taps the picture. "This one, however, is highly toxic. It causes extreme arrhythmia and other heart issues. You mentioned Ms. DuBois had high blood pressure, correct?"

All of us lean in, staring at it, the plant a graceful thing with thin leaves and tiny flowers on long stems.

"Oleander?" I read the entry. My memory of the collection of plants draws a blank. "I don't remember seeing any of that, but perhaps I can sneak into the atrium and check during the ball."

"It might grow outside too," he adds.

I get my phone and snap a picture as a reference. Uncle Odin seems content with that and I tell him I'll pass the information onto Robyn when she gets here. He nods, sniffs at the candles and sighs. "One of my favorites."

After he leaves, I tell the others about Finn's investor. They act as if I've grown a second head and am suggesting they drink poison.

"An investor?" Zelle exclaims with a trace of disgust. "You always said this was our company. Grandma's legacy. Our one rule is to keep it *in the family.*"

I add the coloring to the new batch. "I'm not

suggesting we go with the investor angle, I only want you guys to know it's an option. If we partner with this person, we could get started right away with the remodel, and within a short amount of time, double our showroom space and rearrange this area to make it more efficient. We can knock out that wall over there to increase flow between the workroom and store-room. We might even be able to put in a small bath-room down here, so we could quit running upstairs every time we have to go."

Ruby is thoughtful, but I see in her eyes her heart isn't in it. "It makes sense, businesswise."

Zelle shakes her head adamantly, her gaze flipping between Ruby and me. "Are you kidding? You'd seri-ously consider bringing an outsider into our business?"

"I don't like it," Belle adds.

I reach out and take Zelle's hand. "I'm trying to get us in the black enough that we can afford to hire you and Belle full time."

She squeezes my fingers. "Belle and I are fine."

Belle nods her agreement.

Zelle continues. "We both love our other jobs, and even though we've dreamed for a long time of joining you and Ruby fulltime, we'll be okay. Let's take the expansion and do it right, not bring in strangers simply to do it quick. That's asking for trouble, and you know it. You've preached that to us for years. It worked for Eunice and the women who came after her, including Mom. Why would we change that?"

Because we live in a very different world than they did. "I know." I add the scents, stirring them in well. "But I may have been short-sighted about how long it will take if we don't get a loan or bring on Finn's investor."

"Do you think he's the investor?" Ruby asks.

I'm not the only psychic in the family to be sure. "Could be. Either way, does it matter?"

"I'm willing to wait and I'm sure Belle is as well." Zelle begins pouring the second batch of candles. "Don't worry about us so much, Cinder."

Belle nods, labeling the containers. "The important thing is we stick together, and we run this place the way we want to."

Ruby continues her labeling. "I love your ideas for the expansion, and I'm totally on board with keeping it within the family, no matter how long it takes. I'll throw as much as I can into the remodeling fund."

"I can get more work at the salon, pick up extra events." Zelle finishes off the last candle. "Those pay really well. Thinking about Leo gives me the idea to offer home visits. There are other elderly and house-bound folks in the area who might appreciate it."

I rub the ends of my fingers, sprinkling magic into each jar. "Do you have time?"

"I'll make time. It'll be fun," she assures me.

Ruby leans on the countertop crossing her ankles. "I've actually been thinking about starting a side candy business. That could contribute to the fund."

"That's a fantastic idea." Zelle pushes her long

braid off her shoulder. "I took a plate of candies to the salon today and those women gobbled them up. A couple of them asked me when we were going to start taking orders. I think that could be a great side hustle for you."

"If you want," I tell her, "I could look into converting our kitchen into a commercial one that would pass the county and state health codes. I can rework my layout for the extra floorspace to include a covered display case."

Her eyes light up and I see the businesswoman in her rising to the surface. "Let me think about it. I have to estimate how much time it will take to continually fill a case and keep everything fresh, but it might be doable. I bet Uncle Odin would pitch in."

Zelle winks at her. "You've been keeping up with us stealing all of them."

There's a knock at the shop entrance. "That must be Robyn." I wipe my hands on a towel. "Set the timer." The candles have to set up for twenty minutes before we add the crystals to the tops. "You guys clean up and figure out what we're having for dinner. All this talk about candy has made me hungry. After I speak to Robyn, I'll add the crystals and trim the wicks."

Each of them gives me a quick hug before I head out front.

Robyn tells me she doesn't have time for tea tonight and I notice she still seems as tired as she was the other day. "Rowena Appleton is still claiming innocence and she's lawyered up. We haven't found anything else to suggest she poisoned Janice, so all we have is the circumstantial evidence from her laptop. We have no idea how she got the poison into Janice, and we won't be able to hold her on suspicion much longer. Do you have any theories?"

Administering poison isn't in my repertoire. "Sorry, no. I know this is really stressful for you, and I'll continue to do what I can to help."

"My boss is talking about calling in assistance from the county sheriff's department. Possibly even a detective or two from the big city."

She wipes a hand across her face and tucks a strand of hair behind her ear. She hates the idea of anyone, whether from the county or Atlanta, taking over her case, and I don't blame her.

Her gaze is serious. "Show me what you've got, and please tell me it ties to the maid and this crazy case, Cinder."

What if all of this *doesn't* tie to the case? Worry eats at my stomach, my appetite suddenly gone. "I was at the mansion, fixing a leaky pipe, and discovered a pager hidden under the sink."

One dark brow lifts. "Go on."

When I explain that I dialed the number on the display, her brow lowers in a chastising stare. "You should have called me."

"Probably," I agree, "but listen, there was a man on the other end, and he asked, 'Is everything in place for Saturday?'"

Now both brows rise and hope lights her face. "Okay, this is good." She has me text her the picture of the pager and says she'll try to get a warrant to search the house again, but doubts the judge will give it to her based on that evidence.

I also show her the picture of the oleander from Uncle Odin's book. "Do you remember seeing this plant when you were going through the atrium?"

Her gaze meets mine. "No, but I'm familiar with it. Mama had a few last year. It typically gets too cold here to grow outside, and all but one died during the winter. Mostly, you find them along the coast and down in Florida. Beautiful flowers. And highly toxic."

"Exactly. I'm hoping to get back inside the atrium tomorrow night during the ball and look for it. Would that be enough to get you the warrant?"

She shrugs. "Only if the odd compound they discovered in Janice's stomach matches, but yes, if that happens, that will break the case open for us."

"I'll find it if it's there," I assure her.

"Couldn't you just ask your boyfriend?"

"My boyfriend?" She winks and I give her an admonishing look. "For your information, he's not my boyfriend. I could ask him, but I've already interrogated him so much, I'd rather not."

She gives me a tired smile. "I'm kidding. I'd prefer you don't alert any of them that we're looking into this possibility. Not even Finn."

Meaning, he's still under suspicion. My heart sinks. "You know, if you want me to inspect those shoes, I might be able to determine why Janice was wearing them."

She scrutinizes my face, giving me a dubious gaze. "Look, I know you can do some magickal stuff, but even if you picked up something off the shoes, I can't take it to a judge, nor would it hold up in court. The insight might be appreciated, and if it comes to that, I'll take you up on the offer—especially if it keeps me on the case and outside law enforcement from getting their hands on it—but until I get that desperate, let's go by the book, okay?"

"Of course," I reply.

The dinger goes off and she leaves. I add the citrine gemstone chips to the candle tops, trim the wicks, then I head upstairs for dinner.

CHAPTER

SIXTEEN

The night of the ball, we're excited to see the play, though I'm anxious, too. While Robyn still believes Rowena is guilty, I have doubts, and I'm wondering if we're going to be spending the night with the true killer.

Zelle does my hair, and Matilda my makeup. She's decided she doesn't want to go to the ball, and since I didn't score an invite for her, I'm relieved. She and Odin have made other plans—I'm not sure I want to know what those are, but at least I won't have to keep an eye on her.

McAlister sits on my dressing table, Belle twirling in front of the full-length mirror in one corner, looking for the world like she was born to the garnet gown and matching shoes she's chosen.

Zelle puts the finishing touches on my hair, adding a few sparkling butterfly pins, and Ruby is completely ready. How she did it so fast makes me wonder if she used a bit of magick.

I'm still in my robe, the Zelle's borrowed dress laid out on my bed. I've had to chase Savannah off multiple times, and I'll probably be wearing more cat hair than satin tonight.

Matilda is trying to do my lashes, but I keep blinking, smearing the midnight black mascara under my bottom lids. She's so frustrated, I finally hold out a hand. "Let me take care of this," I suggest.

Using magick, I wipe a hand past my face. The smeared mess disappears, and long, lush eyelashes sprout, a tasteful dark fringe around both eyes.

Matilda sits back, the mascara wand in one hand, the bottle in the other and squints at me. "Why in Valhalla's name didn't you do that in the first place?"

The loss of her magick grates on her nerves, and that's why I don't use mine much around her, especially to replace somethings she's doing manually. "How do I look? Do I pass?"

She huffs and returns the wand to its plastic holder. "Stunning. You might think about wearing makeup more often."

"Why would I do that?"

She playfully slaps my arm at my sarcasm. "Get your dress on."

I stand to grab it and she waves me off. "Not that one."

"That's the one I picked to wear. Zelle agreed, it looks good on me."

She points a finger in the air. "Wait here."

As she disappears through the doorway, my sisters and I exchange a glance and a shrug. "What is she up to?" I whisper.

McAlister chitters from his cage, as if he's in on it. I pull him out and give him a scratch, holding him up to peer into his eyes. I've tried connecting with him psychically a few times, but what I get back always sounds like radio static. He gets an extra biscuit tonight, made with his favorite fruits and veggies, along with a few crushed pieces of high protein cat food—don't tell Savannah—and I hold one in my fingers to let him chew on it. His tiny paws grip the biscuit as he munches away.

Matilda returns with a large box wrapped with a wide red velvet ribbon.

"What is that?" I ask.

With a smirk, she puts it on the bed. "I don't ask for much, but do me a favor and wear this."

She unties the ribbon and my sisters gather round. Before our eyes, a beautiful gold ballgown emerges.

The satin sparkles, the thin straps appear made from crystals.

The dress boutique—this was one I coveted but wouldn't touch because it cost a fortune. It was way too much for me, period—too much money, too much glamour, too much everything, including that skirt!

I freeze, not wanting to hurt her feelings, but knowing I'll feel awkward and completely out of my comfort zone in the stunning gown. I'm not like Ms.

Starling—I hate calling attention to myself. "I don't know what to say, Matilda."

Belle *oohs*, and Ruby smiles. Zelle steps forward, takes the dress from our godmother, and holds it up to me. "It's perfect! How did you know Cinder loved this one?"

Matilda gives us a chiding regard. "I know everything."

More like, she called Mrs. Grimmly and asked.

I touch the shimmering folds that remind me of a golden wedding gown, the satin soft under my fingers. The weight of it is luxurious. A dozen buttons run down the back of the corset; the full skirt goes to the floor. "I've never seen anything more beautiful," I admit.

"Put it on," Matilda demands. "Trust me, it will fit."

That tells me it has magickal properties. If she could still do magick, I'd suspect she'd enchanted it. Since she can't, I wonder who did.

My sisters are watching me, all of them with huge grins and encouragement in their eyes. They are as surprised as I am, so that only leaves Uncle Odin.

Sweet man.

"I don't know..." I bite my lower lip. "It's so extravagant."

"Mom would love to see you in this," Zelle states.

Ruby and Belle nod in agreement.

Hard to argue with the Mom card.

Since my normal attire is worn jeans and casual tshirts, I feel like I'm carrying liquid gold as I take the gown into the bathroom. An odd sense of elation fills my chest and I wonder what it will look like once I have it on.

Matilda knocks at the door and peeks in. "You might need help getting that on."

She's right. Between the weight of the fabric, several layers of tulle under the skirt, and my now shaking hands, it takes both of us to get me into it. The buttons are for decoration, and thankfully, it has a side zipper.

The satin and silk combination hugs my body as my godmother zips me in. I discover pockets and sink my hands into them, testing their depth. *Functional and fashionable*, I think. Maybe this *will* work.

In the mirror, I'm only able to see the top half of the dress, but it's breathtaking in its sheer simplicity and cut. A classy smattering of crystals lines the cleavage, demur and yet breathtaking. The nearly glowing material is like a soft glove, embracing me in a gentle hug.

"You look dazzling," Matilda says, touching the sparkling beadwork around the waist. "Your mother would definitely love this on you."

My eyes tear up and I hug her. "I'm completely blown away."

When I step out from the bathroom, my sisters gasp in unison. Their eyes are big, and so are their smiles.

For the first time in my life, I feel feminine and very

elegant as I sweep over to the full-length mirror. From the top of my coiffed head to the bottom hem of the dress puffed out around me, I'm completely transformed.

Even my bare feet feel dignified and graceful.

"Shoes." Zelle snaps her fingers, as if reading my mind. "You should wear Mom's."

My knee jerk reaction is to say no. I can't wear *those*, not the ones hiding in the back of my closet. They were her wedding shoes, and they should be preserved, especially since they were the last pair she wore.

But when I turn to face the women around me, I see a spark in their eyes that reminds me of her. Happiness, joy, love.

I caress a hand down the skirt. "Shouldn't we keep those shoes where they are?"

Matilda takes my hand. "Your mother would be so proud of you, and happy to see you actually enjoying yourself for once. I know how hard you work to take care of this family, Cinder, and all of us appreciate what you do. Just tonight, can you be a young woman going to a ball in a magickal dress? A breathtaking woman, in fact, honoring her mother by wearing a pair of her shoes?"

"Have fun for once," Ruby encourages.

My other two sisters nod, each of them stepping forward to hug me and echoing Matilda's wish.

"Okay," I relent. "I'll wear the shoes."

Overwhelmed by emotions, several tears slip down

my cheeks when I pull on the wedding shoes, the straps trimmed in a gold thread that matches the dress. Once more I stand before the four women in my life who mean everything to me.

Belle makes me twirl in a circle, and I can't help but laugh. The last time I acted like this was so long ago I've forgotten how it feels. From his cage, McAlister makes a noise that sounds like approval.

A few minutes later, my sisters are ready as well, each of them dressed stylishly, and excited to get to the theater.

Unexpectedly, Nonni sticks her head in the bedroom door and sucks in a breath when she sees the four of us. Her hand goes to her lips and her eyes glisten. "Oh, my girls."

She moves to stand next to Matilda, the two of them sharing a knowing smile. "Sometimes I forget you're all so grown up." Nonni wipes at the corner of one eye. "I've never seen you look more beautiful. I hope you don't mind, but I had to sneak over and see you before you go. Poppi wants a picture."

My paternal grandparents helped raised us, along with Matilda and Uncle Odin, after Mom and Dad died, and we couldn't do without them. We model, adding a goofy one in among the more formal poses, and then Nonni kisses each of us on the cheek. She's wearing a gold scarf around her neck and unties it.

Shaking it out, she drapes the sheer fabric around my shoulders like a shawl. "Have a great time. I expect all of you over for Sunday dinner to tell me every single thing that happens tonight, promise?"

The warmth of the shawl feels like home. We agree and I hug her tightly before we file downstairs. As we walk out to get in the van, we're surprised to find a carriage waiting for us. Finn jumps out to open the door, dressed in a tuxedo.

My breath lodges in my lungs.

"Your carriage awaits, m'ladies," he says, giving us a deep, sweeping bow.

"Where in the world did you get this?" Belle asks.

"Leo Kingsley," he announces. "He happened across this baby a couple of weeks ago and didn't know what to do with it."

"Is that Jasmine and Buttercup?" Ruby wants to know, stepping closer to eye the horses.

"I borrowed them from your grandparents."

Nonni waves at him from the back porch.

He winks at her, then at our godmother. "It was Matilda's idea."

"You?" I ask.

She shrugs self-deprecatingly. "You can't go a fancy ball in that old thing." She hitches a thumb over her shoulder, pointing at the van.

This night keeps getting better. I'm delighted at this over-the-top act and can't keep my eyes off Finn. "What a wonderful surprise."

As my sisters climb in, Finn takes my hand and pulls me aside. He stares into my eyes, the night sky above him shining with stars. "'*If I could write the beauty of your eyes, and in fresh numbers number all your graces, the age to come would say, This poet lies; Such heavenly touches ne'er touch'd earthly faces.'"*

My knees go weak. My eyes well up again. "Are you quoting Shakespeare?"

The horses stamp and snort, ready to go. He nods. "Are you crying?"

My voice is barely above a whisper. "My father used to say that to my mother."

He wipes the tear escaping from my eye and smiles. "Thank you for coming tonight."

I draw the shawl tighter around my shoulders, the chill night air nipping at my skin. "Thank you for inviting me."

He helps me into the carriage, and a moment later, the driver clucks at the horses and away we go.

SEVENTEEN

We arrive at the theater, receiving lots of attention thanks to Finn and the carriage.

Hollywood has come to Story Cove.

There are photographers lining the red carpet the theater has put out for the event. Through the carriage window, I spot Callie speaking to a reporter and signing autographs.

I'm completely self-conscious when cameras start flashing as Finn exits. They illuminate the interior like lightning.

He reaches out a hand for me. A flash hits me square in the face and I freeze, my hand reaching for his but not touching it yet. He's not a star, but his mother is, and he's used to this.

I'm not.

Everything in me wants to draw back, hide from the gathered crowd around the theater's entrance. It seriously does resemble a small-scale Hollywood premiere, complete with a red carpet walkway and people waving and begging Finn for a photo or autograph.

"Cinder." Ruby places a gentle hand on my shoulder. "Prince Charming is waiting."

I gulp. Finn smiles from the curb. "It's okay," he says. "They won't bite."

A nervous laugh bubbles up, choking me. I glance at Zelle and Belle. They both wear huge grins.

"Time to shine," Zelle encourages with a wink.

"Don't worry about us," Belle admonishes. "Go."

I swallow the lump in my throat. I can't breathe and my legs are shaking, even though I'm still seated.

Finn's hand touches mine as he inclines toward me. "I won't let anything happen to you, Cinder Ella Sherwood. You have my word."

I haven't leaned on anyone in a long time. Yes, I have Matilda and Uncle Odin. Nonni and Poppi. I love them all, and I couldn't do without them, but ever since Mom and Dad died, I've been the strong one. The "normal" one. The one they all could depend on to keep life in balance, to protect and love them unconditionally in this crazy, undependable world.

His hand is warm, strong, reassuring. The encouragement in his eyes, as well as my sisters', makes a warm drop of courage surface in my belly. As I grip his hand and scoot forward on the seat, another flash goes off but it doesn't make me flinch. The people on the sidewalk are happy, excited, and seemingly kindhearted. They've come out tonight to support the theater, our new neighbors the Starlings, and the town.

Gathering the folds of my gown with my free hand, and feeling the shoes on my feet tingle with Mom's love, the warmth inside my belly grows. I manage a smile at Finn, his strong hand guiding me.

My legs are a bit uncooperative, but I draw a reassuring breath as my first shoe finds the sidewalk. Finn steadies me as I set the other down, my body quivering. He draws me close, one hand waving at the gathered crowd. A cheer goes up.

Folks yell questions, a young girl in pink tulle begs for a selfie with him. He leans in, lets her take the photo, and signs a playbook, all the while keeping me near.

Ruby and the twins pass by, each squeezing my arm in solidarity as Finn gives the crowd what they want.

By the time he and I make it inside, I'm smiling. Several of the fans complimented my dress, hair, and makeup. One reporter is bold enough to ask if Finn and I are serious. I pretended not to hear that one.

"See? That wasn't so bad," Finn says. More fans press toward us, a repeat of requests for autographs and selfies. He's gracious to each of them.

"Speak for yourself," I reply, keeping a smile in place. I scan these closest to us and am relieved not to see Jason. "I don't know how you and your mom do this."

Ms. Starling is already in her private box, waving

to the crowd and signing autographs for those who make their way up to the balcony with their playbills. She's in the height of her glory and seems to love it. Finn and I join her, Belle, Zelle, and Ruby in the coveted box seats in the front row, compliments of our hostess.

As we enjoy the first two acts, Ms. Starling uses a small pen light to list notes in her playbook, occasionally making a soft grunt or other noise in her throat as the actors move through their lines. At the end of the second act, the lights come up for a short break, and Ms. Starling hastily leaves the box, letting us know she needs to go talk to Don Louis about Bonnie, the woman playing her role of Katie.

Finn reaches over and lightly touches my hand. "What do you think?"

"It's pretty good," I admit. I've been eyeing the shoes Bonnie is wearing. "The glass slippers look identical to your mom's."

"She donated a copy to the theater."

"A copy?"

He traces one of my fingers with his, a gentle touch that makes my pulse race. "On movie sets they have duplicates of props. I think they made at least half a dozen of the famous Glass Slippers, and Mother has three or four pairs, including the originals. Those are the ones she claims are magic." He makes air quotes around 'magic' before returning to caress my hand.

Thanks to his touch, it's hard for me to think straight. "I thought the police still had the originals."

"It's hard to tell the difference, and Mother was hoping to get those returned, but at least she wasn't planning on auctioning that pair."

"She wasn't? I saw the place marker for them in the ballroom the other day."

"She's auctioning one of the extras." He takes my hand and turns it palm up, tracing his thumb over the lines in the center. "I hope she's not giving Don Louis an earful."

My mouth feels dry and I lick my lips, watching Finn's thumb. "Do you think she's happy with the play? She was making a lot of notes, and a lot of disgusted noises."

He chuckles. "Even if it was perfect, she would find faults. She lives for this kind of thing, and she really misses her acting days. This play and the ball have brought her back to life. It's good to see. I wish the biographer's death didn't overshadow everything."

To me, Ms. Starling doesn't seem concerned about Janice's demise. "Are they sending another biographer to finish the book?"

"Nobody yet. The publishing house is concerned about all the publicity, and it's a two-edge sword. They'd love to rush something to press to capitalize on the new attention on her, but on the other hand, Janice's family may sue them if the police determine it's a homicide. They're claiming fault could lie with both the publisher and Mother. I expect we'll be served papers soon."

"That's terrible."

A shrug. "We've been sued before, mostly because she's famous."

He's so cavalier, I figure they know how to handle such a thing, but it makes me want to cast a protection spell over both of them.

"Have you given anymore thought to the investor angle?" he asks.

"I took the offer to my sisters, and I'm sorry, but that's off the table. We'd rather go slow with the expansion and keep it in the family. I hope you understand."

Disappointment briefly flits over his features. "I don't blame you. If there's anything I can do, such as donate some of my time to help with the architectural plans, you'll let me know?"

Since we need a professional to sign off on the expansion to take to the town board, I'm delighted with this offer. "Our town doesn't have many building codes, but the county does, so that'll be quite helpful. I probably can't afford your hourly rates, but maybe we can work something out?"

"Are you bribing me?"

"I'm willing to barter for soap, lotion, or candles. Lifetime supply?"

He winks, his thumb moving to my wrist and rubbing along the jumping pulse there. "Throw in a few of Ruby's candies, and you've got a deal."

The overhead lights flicker, alerting people the break is over. Ms. Starling returns just as the lights begin to fall, and Finn threads his fingers through mine.

As the third act comes to an end, I have to admit the play is good. The emotions and the happy ending tug at my heart strings. I'm sure the original movie deserves its classic status.

The curtain drops and loud applause echoes through the high-ceilinged playhouse, Ms. Starling rises to her feet and many in the crowd applaud her as well.

The cast comes out to take a bow, each one of them stepping forward one at a time to receive individual praise. Finally, it's Bonnie's turn. From the center of the lineup, she steps forward, but sways slightly.

With the standing ovation and hooting, whistling, and cheering going on, I expect her to be full of smiles and wave at the crowd. Instead she looks ashen, jittery, a hand going to her stomach.

The actor who played her love interest, the prince, steps to her elbow. This seems to steady her, and after a moment, she sweeps an apprehensive bow. When she straightens, she clasps hold of him and staggers. The glass slippers sparkle under the bright lights.

He says something to her, and she nods, forcing herself to face the crowd once more. He acts as though he's reluctant to release her elbow, yet doesn't want to infringe on her receiving praise, since she's the star of the show.

He takes half a step back to put her solely in the

spotlight again, and the actress smiles, raising a hand to the crowd. More cheering, a few loud whistles.

Still incredibly pale and ghoulish in her stage makeup, her smile falters. The hand falls to her stomach once more. Her eyes flutter up in her head.

The next thing we know, Bonnie falls to the stage.

CHAPTER

EIGHTEEN

Rumors fly about the cursed shoes, but the EMTs assure Don Louis it looks like a straightforward case of exhaustion. The actress is whisked away to the hospital, and the director, cast, and Ms. Starling insist the ball will go on.

My sisters and I, along with Finn, arrive at the mansion in short order, determined not to let the event cloud our excitement.

We're greeted at the door by Callie, who apparently has taken over at least this part of the housekeeping duties for tonight. She's changed since the play and now wears a rich aqua sequined number that hugs her frame. She seems rather happy to see all of us, and I wonder if she's acting. Or maybe, like Finn, she has so few friends here that she's truly happy to see familiar faces.

In the ballroom, music swells and fills the high-ceilinged room. The bartender is setting out rows of specialty blue-tinged drinks with miniature fruit kabobs in them, and the auction items reside on the table along the side of the room. As Finn stated, a copy of the glass slippers are present. Even close up, I see no distinction from the originals. Turning on my second sight, I register the same odd aura as well, only slightly weaker.

More tables and chairs have been added since the dinner party, and people mingle and dance on the large floor. Finn and I join his mom, Callie, the Dickenses, and Don Louis at one of the tables. The DJ does a great job switching between fast pop songs, and slower more romantic melodies.

I watch my sisters having fun and feel a particular joy. Giving them this night makes up for a lot of holidays, birthdays, and other life events that they've missed out on with our parents. I know that we're adults, but there's never true closure when you lose your parents, especially so young, and I hope this extravagant affair will give them memories to hang onto forever.

Finn and I enjoy dancing and flirting, and he asks me if I want to bid on any of the silent auction items. I decline, and he brings me one of the blue drinks from the bar.

Ms. Starling disappears, Lucinda Dickens with her. Most likely hitting the guest bathroom, which I hope is functioning well.

As the night wears on, I see Elsa rushing in and out several times, checking on the bartender. The chef is dressed up and looks nice, and I let her know, but all she does is give a derisive snort. "Just don't spill any liquor on your dress tonight," she warns, and I can't tell if she's joking with me or criticizing my clumsiness from the dinner.

At one point while Finn and I are doing the chicken dance with a bunch of others, Callie says something to the bartender and the look on his face gives me pause. After the dance is over, I beg off from Finn, telling him I need a glass of ice water. he offers to get it for me.

"Why don't you check on your mom?" I suggest, since she's still gone. "I can get the water. I don't want to hog you all to myself. This is her big night."

He kisses my temple. "I'll be back in a few minutes. You still owe me another dance."

I head to the bar, and as I approach, Callie sees me coming. Her face is grim. She passes by, hustling away, and I reach out to touch her arm. "Is everything okay?"

She hesitates then says. "Fine. Enjoy."

Watching her go, I step to the bar and fan myself. "Ice water, please."

He doesn't meet my eyes, taking the towel from his shoulder and throwing it next to the sink. "Bar's closed. I'm on a break."

My ears prick at the sound of his voice, and I stand dumbfounded as I watch him follow Callie, now exiting the room at the back door. A cold chill runs over my skin, and I remind myself that I couldn't hear him clearly over the background noise of the music.

But in my bones, I know that voice.

He's the man on the other end of that phone number.

I need to get to the atrium and check for that plant, but a part of me wants to shadow him and see where he's going.

Hesitation burns in my veins. Glancing around for my sisters, I spot Belle chatting with a friend from the play. Zelle and Ruby are nowhere to be seen, and I wonder if they've snuck off to the bathroom, or maybe to check out the beautiful mansion.

Ms. Starling returns, her arm tucked into Finn's side, and they're engaged in a heavy discussion. I skirt the dancers and head out, following on the heels of Callie and the bartender.

By the time I reach the hall leading to the east wing, Callie's disappeared, but I hear the heavy steps of the bartender. Hanging back so he won't hear me, my mouth is definitely dry and I'm beginning to sweat.

As I move through what seems like a maze, we go right then left, then left again. It's only when I see the foyer and the double staircases that I'm able to re-orient myself.

Where are he and Callie going? Is she in danger from him?

If he were really on a break, wouldn't he head outside for a smoke or fresh air, or maybe to the bathroom?

I hug close to the wall at the rear of the formal sitting room that I was in several days ago, and intuition tells me the answer... He's on his way to the atrium.

Perfect. Maybe I can kill two birds with one stone. Make sure Callie's all right and search for the oleander.

Sure enough, by the time I reach the glassed-in greenhouse, he's ducked inside. The double doors are cracked open, and the overhead lights are off, but there's enough decorative lighting around the large spacious interior, I can see the various tables and displays of plants without too much trouble.

Allowing my eyes to adjust to the dimness, I'm thankful for the moon overhead shining down through the glass roof.

I'm sneaking in the cracked doorway when I hear the man's voice. "Did you get them?"

Ducking behind a large group of tall plants, one of them resembling a tree, I lean my ear toward the sound and hear Callie's reply. "These are the real ones."

Using a hand, I part layers of branches to sneak a peek. Sure enough, I see his back. One of his arms reaches for what she's handing him. The soft moonlight glitters off a pair of shoes as she holds them up, turning them this way and that. "They'll be worth millions."

A hard pit feels stuck in my throat. Are those the *real* Glass Slippers? Is she stealing from Ms. Starling?

She tucks them into a dark bag before I can send out my psychic sensor, then hands the whole thing to him. I don't have time to escape before they're walking toward me.

Crouching, I shift deeper into the collection of plants, my gold dress a beacon under the moonlight if they see me. The skirt catches on an ivy branch, leaves and tiny twigs smack at my cheek. All I can do, as I hear them quickly closing in, is stop moving and hold my breath.

Instinct makes me drop into the voluminous skirt, hiding my upper body in it and waving my fingers above my head. Magick descends like an umbrella over me.

As I peer from the folds of material, they scurry past, neither looking in my direction. Pulse skittering, I breathe a huge sigh of relief once they've exited and I hear the click of the door shutting behind them.

From my pocket emerges a buzzing that startles me so bad I jump and knock into the tree. The plant and I both topple, soil flying and getting on my dress. Huffing, I get to my feet, brushing at the dirt I see staining the satin. I swear under my breath.

My phone buzzes again, and I hastily dig through the folds of the skirt. I need to call Robyn and alert my sisters. I don't know if this has anything to do with Janice's death, but there's a crime that's about to be perpetrated.

When I look at the onscreen ID, I thank the universe. *Perfect timing.* I run to the door, trying to keep Callie and the bartender in sight, but they've already vanished into the cavernous house.

Still, I keep my voice low. "Robyn! I'm so glad it's you. You have to get to the mansion ASAP. They're stealing Ms. Starling's shoes. The real ones. The ones Janice wore must be a copy. You need to get here now."

"Okay, okay, calm down. Listen, the actress from the play just died. It wasn't heat exhaustion or over-work. My bet is poisoning. I'm on the way to question everyone. Don't let anyone leave. Everyone's a suspect, so protect yourself, you hear?"

"Oh no!"

"Yes, now stay calm and I'll be there in a few minutes."

The moment we hang up, I text my sisters, alerting them. Pocketing the phone, I hustle out of the atrium and search for the two culprits.

Unfortunately, they've disappeared into thin air. I'm retracing my steps to the ballroom in order to alert Finn and his mom when I hear the unmistakable foot-falls of the bartender.

I wind my way back to the foyer, but realize he's headed toward the back of the mansion. And then I see Callie emerging from the guest bathroom.

She no longer has the bag with the shoes, and I'm suddenly suspicious of the hiding place where I found the pager. I duck into the shadows under the steps.

Callie catches up with the bartender. "I'll retrieve them and meet you outside in ten minutes. There's something I need from upstairs before I leave."

"We need to go now."

"Not until I get what's mine."

He grunts and I hear his footsteps fade away. Callie passes by and goes up the massive staircase.

In a flash I race for the bathroom thankful to find it empty. It wears an out-of-order sign on the doorknob.

Inside, I jiggle the vanity drawer out and see the pager is missing. The stains that I saw on it—I glance down at my soiled-stained skirt. The pager... was it in the bag of potting soil next to Janice's body?

My intuition is in overdrive and I see the scene playing out in my head. At some point, that pager made contact with soil from the atrium, and whether or not Janice surprised Callie, or another altercation happened, it's possible it was stashed here afterward.

Now, instead of the pager, the bag containing the infamous shoes lies inside.

I pull on the draw string and stick my hand in. The shoes feel cool to the touch, and there's definitely a magickal vibration to them. I pause—if these are the real Glass Slippers, are they indeed cursed? If I put one on, what will happen to me?

I know better than to play with cursed objects, but the magick coming off this pair is not dark. In fact, it's almost the opposite...it feels charmed.

All night, the emotions from my mother's shoes have been filling me up, but now I remove them and wiggle my bare feet in the plush carpeting. I eye the glass slippers, taking a deep breath and sending a shot of protective magick through my system, just in case.

Holding one to the bottom of my foot to measure the difference in size, I cringe. The shoes are at least a full size smaller, but for the sake of determining once and for all whether they're cursed, and if they can tell me anything about what's going on in this mansion, I'll have to squeeze my feet into them.

Hanging onto the vanity, I tug on the first, and experience a rush of adrenaline. Something else too. Dots dance in the edges of my vision, but I force my other foot into the second and open my psychic abilities wide.

Blurs of colors, textures, and sounds is all I get at first. I hear applause, feel elated. I'm suddenly not me, but someone else, looking out over a crowd of people dressed in tuxedoes and glamorous dresses.

Just as the first revelation hits, the bathroom door flies open. Jerking me out of the vision, there stands Callie Lane.

As startled as I am, she meets my eyes before her wide-eyed gaze falls to my feet. Peeking out from under the hem of my dress, the shoes sparkle.

"You," she says with hatred burning in her voice.

Before I can move, she draws a gun from her handbag. "I should have known you were nothing but a small-town busy-body."

She points the gun at me.

CHAPTER

NINETEEN

Bits and pieces of what Callie's been doing flicker through my mind, thanks to the shoes. They have magickal properties far beyond what I've experienced before. Janice never wore them, but Callie did.

I hate to stop the flow of information, but with a gun aimed at my head, I don't have much choice.

"Take them off." She takes a step closer. "Now."

Keeping one hand on the vanity, I carefully slide off the left, then wrestle with the right. That one is stuck. "I've alerted the police," I tell her, fighting with it. "You won't get away with any of this."

She cocks her head, chin out. "Get away with what?"

The right shoe gives reluctantly, and holding onto the flimsy strap, I use my free hand to adjust my skirt. As I do, I slip my fingers inside the pocket holding my cellphone. A little magick and the phone dials Robyn.

Since she was the last person I spoke with, the simple spell will re connect us once more with ease. I'm not sure the speaker will work through the layers of fabric, but I can hope.

Toying with the shoe, I try to buy time. "I know what you did, I just don't know why."

She's calm, offering a humorless chuckle. "You don't know anything."

"I know you're going to steal these shoes and sell them, and finger Tiffany for Janice's death. At least that was your intention, wasn't it? So far, it hasn't worked."

She curls a lip, but still seems calm. "Rowena, God bless her. She followed Tiffany around like a fan girl all the time, and all the things I planned got turned on their ear by her and that stupid biographer."

"So, you're letting Rowena take the fall for poisoning Janice. Was it oleander? Did you poison Bonnie too, trying to throw suspicion on the shoes again?"

One brow quirks as if she's impressed at my deductions, but she doesn't answer my questions. Instead, she asks one of her own. "Are you a real witch?"

The question takes me off guard. "Who told you that?"

A knowing smile is her answer. "Have you told Finn? Obviously not, or you wouldn't be here."

"What do you mean?"

"Oh *puulease*. Do you really think he'd date

someone like you? Even if you weren't a witch, you're a cute distraction for him, that's all. He's dated actresses, models, the cream of the crop. What do you think he sees in a small-town girl like you who can't even afford a decent gown for the ball?"

My heart sinks, but I stiffen my spine. She's a good actress, and I sense she's trying to distract me, but the dig about the ballgown is too low. Story Cove may not be L.A., but this gown rocks. "How did you get her to eat it? Janice and the oleander?"

Distraction foiled, she's grown tired of the game. "Does it matter? You're about to die. Give me the shoes."

Thanks to the charmed pair and my psychic abilities, I've seen a pill bottle with Janice's name on it. I suspect Callie slipped dried oleander inside a few of the capsules. I remove the hand with my phone out of my pocket and set the device on the vanity, sliding it back as if it's of no consequence. At the same time, I raise the shoe I'm holding into the air—a different kind of distraction, but effective.

As expected, her gaze tracks the shoe with barely a glance at the phone. I've turned it upside down so she can't see it's connected, and I'm hoping the speakers pick up our conversation well enough for Robyn. "I've told the others everything I know," I tell her, "so if you kill me, you'll still be charged with murder."

She takes a step forward, eyes lit with vengeful spite. "That biography should've been about *me*. This whole thing should have been. Tiffany took my chance to be famous forty years ago, and I've never forgotten it."

I fiddle with the shoe again, keeping her attention. "You're righting a wrong by killing Janice and stealing these?"

"Once that biographer showed up, I thought maybe, just maybe, Tiff might give me a paragraph or two in her story. Mention how I've stayed all these years to help her, patiently listening to her whine and moan about her dwindling stardom. Being forced to support her schemes to get in the spotlight again. I'm the one who's sacrificed! I'm the one who deserves the spotlight."

I lean a hip against the vanity, casually looking down at my feet and wiggling my toes as if we're having a normal conversation, and a somewhat boring one at that. "It seems you've actually brought her more notoriety and publicity than if you'd left Janice alone."

The gun moves closer to my face, gaining my attention once more. It's trembling in her grip, but I'm not sure if it's because she's uncomfortable at the idea of pulling the trigger or because her anger is getting the best of her. "What do you know? Your generation has no idea what it was like forty years ago. All you have to do is put a video on YouTube, and you're discovered." Her face contorts. "I worked my backside off to become a Hollywood star, and look what it got me. I've always played second fiddle to her, and I'm sick of it. It's my turn to have a mansion and staff...and some peace from *her*."

"Why not kill Tiffany then?"

One corner of her lip tilts. "The night's not over yet."

A cold chill runs down my spine. "How are you going to explain all of this? You can't sell the shoes on the open market without drawing attention to yourself."

"If Tiffany dies, pieces of her memorabilia become mine. At least I *was* going to get them, until she came up with the silent auction idea to support your theater." Her voice hitches, this performance worthy of an Oscar. The copied shoes must have been designated for her originally. "Finn doesn't care about any of it, but she knew how much it meant to me, and she changed her will anyway."

As she's speaking, I wiggle my left fingers to temporarily disable the gun without her knowing. The spell won't last long, but it may be enough for me to—

As the magick soars, the door opens, pommeling Callie and propelling her at me.

The spell hits Finn instead. I watch in horror as he drops like a rock, eyes going wide.

Great. I've just disabled my potential boyfriend.

Who apparently doesn't like witches.

"Sorry!" I yell as I release the shoe and grab Callie's wrist, aiming the gun toward the ceiling.

She fights, but she's still in heels and I'm not. One of her ankles twists as I wrestle with her, causing the gun to fire. The bullet shatters the top of the mirror over the sink.

Glass shards rain down on us and we shriek, throwing our arms up to protect our faces.

Finn breaks through my spell and attacks. I whack Callie in the head with the shoe, and Finn disarms her when she falls to the floor. Behind him, the door opens once again, admitting Tiffany.

"What in the world is going on in here?"

I'm struggling to get to my feet and not step on glass. Callie is woozy, but conscious. She screeches at Tiffany. "She's trying to steal the shoes!"

Finn takes the gun and puts it in his belt at the small of his back, then steadies me with a hand. "Your friend is the one doing that," I correct. "And she killed Janice."

Tiffany becomes one hundred percent actress, throwing her hands over her heart and exclaiming, "What? How dare you! I've given you everything! You're no friend of mine, you black-hearted ninny!"

Heart hammering, I'm about to sink into Finn, when I see the bartender approach behind Tiffany. "Look out!"

He throws a beefy arm around her neck and begins to walk her out backward from the room, his other hand raising a weapon and pointing it at me and Finn. He keeps his gaze fastened on Finn while he speaks to Callie. "Get the shoes. Let's go."

"Release my mother." Finn reaches down and grabs Callie by her dress, yanking her up. "Callie's not going anywhere with you and neither are the shoes."

The gun turns on Tiffany, pointing at her temple. "Shut up or your mother dies."

I raise my hands in surrender. "There's no reason to kill anyone. Let's make a trade." My voice shakes as does the rest of me. "Her for the shoes. The two of you can still get out of here before the police arrive."

I know he has no intention of letting Tiffany go— she's his ticket out. Callie begs him to help her. Finn takes the gun from his waistband, flashing it. "You're in no position to make demands."

"Nobody move." I contemplate using magick, but my fingers are trembling so badly I'm afraid of it backfiring.

The bartender yells at Finn to release Callie, and Callie screams at me for ruining everything. Intuition tells me I have no choice. Things are about to go really, really bad.

Magick it is.

I twitch my hands, and the bartender's gun jerks out of his, hovering in the air over to me before dropping to the floor. He shoves Tiffany and she sprawls to the ground with a shriek, one hand landing on the right shoe.

With unexpected grace and speed, she rises to her knees, twists, and smacks him with it. The heel clobbers him in the groin and he buckles, a surprised expression frozen on his face.

In the hallway, I hear Robyn shout. "Stop! Put your hands up!"

"Might take a minute," I tell her as she rushes in and sees him bent over gasping.

Finn supports his mother as she gains her feet and she lifts the shoe to hit the guy again, but Finn stops her. He gently tugs her away from the bartender and Callie, tucking both of us close as Robyn and her team arrest them.

CHAPTER

TWENTY

The clock in the town square chimes midnight as Finn escorts me home. After giving our statements to Robyn and the police, he sent my sisters off in the carriage, and we ended up walking.

The sky overhead twinkles with stars and the moon shines down on us. The sidewalk is cold under my bare feet, but I've had enough of heels, for a long, long time.

In my free hand, my mother's shoes dangle from my fingers. I've always thought my gift of being able to step into people's shoes and know things about them was the weirdest thing ever. Tonight, it helped me unravel a murder mystery, and for that I'm grateful.

Being able to put my feet in Mom's shoes is truly a blessing, and I'm grateful for that too, even though I wish she was still here.

Finn's fingers tentatively intertwine with mine,

and he tucks me close, his warmth welcome. The soil stains on my dress have already disappeared. Uncle Odin knows me well—his enchantment on the gown must include keeping me spot-free. Not an easy task, even with magick.

I told Robyn what I picked up from the shoes about the oleander in Janice's pill bottle. Before we left, she informed us the bartender, using an alias, is a wanted criminal.

Max Turgle, a former bodyguard Callie employed at the height of her brush with stardom, and who left her after her failure at a Hollywood career, was her lover at one point. He came back into her life recently, convincing her it was time to get revenge on Tiffany and reclaim what should have been hers all along.

Before we left, Callie and Max were turning on each other, each blaming one another for their situations in life. The only thing they agreed on was Tiffany being the reason neither ever made it big.

Finn's mom is handling it all pretty well, and he's assured me she'll be talking about this night for the rest of her life. As we walk, television vans and news crews from other towns race past us toward Millionaires Row. My little town is going to be famous.

As the last echo of the bell tolls through the night air, I lean my head on Finn's shoulder. We're a few blocks from the Enchanted Candle & Soap Company, our evening coming to a dramatic end.

Once there, we pause in front of the door, face to face. He smiles at me, the endearing, wayward lock of his hair falling across his forehead. "I can't thank you enough for what you did tonight. You saved my mother, and I'm forever in your debt. Whatever you want, it's yours."

What I want in this moment is for him to take me in his arms, to never leave. I don't know what the future holds, with him living in Atlanta, but that's to worry about when the sun rises. "I'm glad I could help."

"Are you going to tell me how you disarmed Turgle from across the room?"

I bite my lower lip and brush at his hair. "Let's just say it was magick."

"Magick, huh?" He chucks my chin with his crooked finger. "We should probably talk about that in more depth one of these days. There's so much I need to learn about you."

"A little mystery in a relationship is a good thing."

"Can I ask for an official date now? You have to stop turning me down, you're damaging my ego."

"Yes."

His eyebrows disappear behind the lock of hair. "Yes? Really?"

I offer a big smile. "We have a couple of strikes against us, so no guarantees, but one date can't hurt. Besides, you make me laugh. We have fun. I haven't had a lot of that in my life since my parents died. My sisters are always telling me it's important."

"You're not just buttering me up so I help you with your plans for the shop?"

"Do you care?" I counter slyly.

A laugh and he rubs my upper arms under the shawl with his hands. They're irresistibly warm. "Not really. My mission was to keep asking until you caved. You're a tough cookie to crack."

"You just want more candy," I tease.

A grin. "There is that..."

"There's one condition with the date."

His head tips back and he stares up at the moon. "I knew it was too easy."

When his gaze returns, I see humor dancing in his eyes. "Hit me with it."

"I get to pick the place and what we do."

"That's it?"

If he only knew what I'm planning. I give my evil laugh. "That's it," I assure him.

"Anything you want," he says brushing my lips with his. "I want you to be happy, Cinder."

TWENTY-ONE

A few days later, life is somewhat back to normal. Ruby and I are making soaps, Nonni adding botanicals to them. We shared Sunday dinner with her and Poppi at the farmhouse, and gathered eggs and the last of the gourds from her garden.

Robyn has successfully wrapped up the case—Callie intended to frame Tiffany for Janice's death, but things didn't quite go as she'd hoped. The capsules were the means by which Callie administered the dried oleander to Janice, and when Bonnie complained about feeling tired the night of the play, Callie gave her a couple too, out of spite it seems, claiming they were energy boosting supplements Tiffany took all the time. Apparently, Callie didn't have the guts to kill Tiffany, but she had no qualms about ruining the role of Katie for both Rowena and Bonnie, and destroying Tiffany's dreams of taking the screenplay to Hollywood once more.

Zelle and Belle are going through a stack of the books we found in the hidden room, deciding which to keep and what soap recipes to try in the coming months. I've voted for a ginger and lemon combo that makes me think of summer.

After the holidays, business will slow and that's a great time for us to experiment. The twins are using sticky notes to mark recipes, and reading parts of her journal out loud as we work.

The room is filled with the refreshing smell of eucalyptus and mint, and I think again about the expansion, and how it can't come soon enough.

"I want to offer one more time," I announce, "about the investor option. My intuition tells me it's Finn, or maybe even Mr. Kingsley." I wink at Belle. "We could get the remodel done and be up and running, bringing you two"—I point to her and Zelle with a eucalyptus branch—"on board full-time in a matter of months, rather than a year or two."

"What's this about an investor?" Nonni asks.

I fill her in on the details, but I see in her face she knows that's not the choice my sisters will pick.

Ruby begins pouring the melted soap base into the molds. "Our great-great grandmother didn't build this company overnight, and we'll get the expansion done in a reasonable timeframe."

Zelle doesn't even look up from the journal. "I already told you my opinion."

Belle glances at me and nods. "Ditto."

She reaches over Jayne laying at her feet to grab a book from her stack. She holds one up in the air. "These are genuine antiques and may be worth something. I'm sure Mr. Kingsley can appraise them and tell me which ones. He may know people who will buy them."

"Whatever we sell goes in the fund," Zelle finishes. She looks up, wiggling the pencil in her fingers. "I've booked two more private events for this fall. It's good money and I'm putting all of it toward the expansion. Plus," she continues, "I'm selling some of my designer clothes and shoes. I figure between all of those things, I can add at least a couple of thousand to the bottom line."

I want to hug them. Nonni catches my eye from across the table and winks, "Poppi and I have a few antiques that this Kingsley fellow might be interested in. We're ready to downsize a bit. Belle?" My sister peeks up from her book. "Do you think you could arrange for him to come and look at what we've got and tell us if anything is of value?"

Belle grins. "I'll see what I can do."

Ruby draws the next soap form toward her. "I took samples of my candy to the bakery, and they're willing to buy a selection to test market. I can use their kitchen at night when the bakers aren't there to make up the candies in bulk. I have to split the profits fifty-fifty with them, but the rest we can use."

Between all of that and the fact Tiffany has given

me credit for rescuing her the night of the ball, which has gone viral, her many fans have sent thanks. Orders over the internet have doubled.

If it keeps up, we may be working around the clock to keep up with them, and I've already had to purchase more supplies, but this is the first step toward making our dream come true. "You guys are awesome. Even without an investor, I have the feeling our expansion and remodel is going to happen soon."

Matilda strolls in. "Did someone say I'm awesome?"

From her perch near the window, Savannah yawns audibly. This draws a laugh from all of us, and Matilda puts an arm across my shoulders. "I have some money stashed away."

This is not a surprise, but I am shocked at the confession. "Figured you'd be broke after buying me that dress."

She sets her mug on the table. "I will add to the fund, since you give me free room and board. Seems only fair."

Nonni winks at me again, and I have the feeling she's been riding Matilda about her contributions to the family and shop.

"Also," Matilda continues, "I'm going to start teaching magick workshops. Already saw a gal about it over in Magnolia Springs. She's got a group of witch wanna-bes. I'm gonna help them find their inner femi-nine warrior."

My sisters and I exchange worried glances. "Do you think that's wise?"

A scathing look crosses her face and she snaps her fingers. A set of curing candles under the window light up, flames dancing. "Got my mojo back, thanks to my visit to Asgard with Odin last night."

So that's what they were up to. "The curse is lifted?" Belle asks, hopeful.

Our godmother gives a dismissive shrug, then waves her hand, putting out the flames. The wicks are unburned, and I'm grateful for that, since I'd hate to have to redo the batch. "Better than ever."

Uncle Odin appears with a plate of Ruby's candies and announces it's time for a break. No one argues and we descend like vultures, each grabbing our favorites.

By the time we're done with the abundance of orders, I'm tired, but still have a bulk portion of body butter to whip up. I sit on the workroom table with McAlister for a few minutes, enjoying his antics after the others have gone to bed.

My mind is alive with ideas for the remodel, and the new products we're going to carry. I grab my sketchbook and list one in particular I'm excited about.

Finn shows up, and I let him in. He's carrying a blue box wrapped with a pretty white bow and hands it to me. "From Mother. They're not the originals, but you should still be able to get decent money for them for your project."

I undo the ribbon and lift the lid. A pair of glass

slippers resides inside, a soft glow of enchantment oozing from them. I assume they're one of the many copies Tiffany owns.

Smiling, I laugh. "These are perfect, but I'm not selling them."

"Don't tell me you're under their spell now too."

Playfully, I smack his arm. The glow seems to vibrate. "Better than that. Today, I came up with an idea for a line of enchanted candles called Happily Ever After. One will feature a glass slipper, and I'll use these on the display to promote them."

His blue eyes study my face. "You're not scared of the curse?"

I can't tell for sure if he's kidding or not.

Rubbing one of the shoes, I shake my head. "Not at all. In fact, I believe your mother's 'cursed' shoes are actually charmed."

"Charmed?"

I've been reading through my great-grandmother's book about curses and charms, and I realized the odd sensation I kept getting from Tiffany's shoes—the real pair—is the opposite of what everyone assumed. They took on a life of their own and sensed Tiffany's basic goodness. "I believe they were actually keeping her safe from the bad luck following Callie around. Your mom thrived and grew successful, while Callie's underlying jealousy and rage kept her from ever becoming a true star."

His eyes narrow good-naturedly. "You *have* fallen under their spell."

"The only spell I'm under is yours." I lean into him, enjoying the feel of his arms going around me. "Let's just say, the glass slippers have brought me luck too."

This he understands, hugging me tighter. "I'm the lucky one," he declares.

I rest my head on his shoulder. "I wish you didn't have to go back to Atlanta."

"About that...?"

Inclining my head to look up at him, I feel a tingle of psychic awareness. My heart races. "Yes?"

"I'm going to try working from here three days a week. If all goes according to plan, I may move my entire firm here."

"Wow, that's wonderful."

A shrug. "Being the spoiled, rich son of a famous actress has its perks."

I pinch his side and he laughs. "Sounds like we'll have time for more dates."

"On one condition," he teases.

"Deal," I say. "Whatever it is, I'm in."

"I was hoping you'd say that. If I move here, I'm not leaving. You're stuck with me."

Then, in the midst of curing soaps, late-night sketches, and dreams for the future, he kisses me.

Having found my true Prince Charming, I kiss him back.

I SURE HOPE **you enjoyed this story and I'd love to hear from you!**

Sign up for my Cozy Clues Mystery Newsletter and be the FIRST to learn about new releases, sales, behind-the-scenes trivia about the book characters, pictures of my pets, and coloring pages and news *From the Cauldron With Godfrey blog.*

****Ready for more magical adventures with the Sherwood Sisters?**
Belle, Sister Witches of Story Cove is next!

Books, magick, and a beastly mystery will create havoc in Belle's enchanted world! A fairytale retelling of Beauty & the Beast!

Books talk to me. Literally. It's the best kind of magick I know.

If only book aficionado Leo Kingsley would open up to me, too.
READ NOW

READY FOR MORE MAGICK?

Don't miss the next exciting adventure! Sign up for Nyx's Cozy Clues Mystery Newsletter.

And check out these magical stories!

Sister Witches Of Raven Falls Mystery Series

Sister Witches of Raven Falls Special Collection

Of Potions and Portents
Of Curses and Charms
Of Stars and Spells
Of Spirits and Superstition

Confessions of a Closet Medium Cozy Mystery Series

Confessions of a Closet Medium Special Collection

Pumpkins & Poltergeists
Magic & Mistletoe
Hearts & Haunts
Vows & Vengeance
Cupcakes & Corpses
Tea Leaves & Troubled Spirits

Sister Witches of Story Cove (Formerly Once Upon a Witch) Cozy Mystery Series
Coming Fall 2022

Cinder
Belle
Snow
Ruby
Zelle

ABOUT THE AUTHOR

USA Today Bestselling Author Nyx Halliwell who grew up on TV shows like *Buffy the Vampire Slayer* and *Charmed*.

She loves writing stories as much as she loves baking and crafting. She believes in magick and that we each carry it inside us.

She enjoys binge-watching mystery shows with her hubby and reading all types of stories involving magic and animals.

Connect with Nyx today and see pictures of her pets, be the first to know about new books and sales, and find out when Godfrey, the talking cat, has a new blog post! Receive a FREE copy of the Whitethorne Book of Spells and Recipes by signing up for her newsletter http://eepurl.com/gwKHB9

CONNECT WITH NYX TODAY!

Website: nyxhalliwell.com

Email: nyxhalliwellauthor@gmail.com
Bookbub https://www.bookbub.com/profile/nyx-halliwell
Amazon amazon.com/author/nyxhalliwell
Facebook: https://www.facebook.com/NyxHalliwellAuthor/

Sign up for Nyx's Cozy Clues Mystery Newsletter and be the FIRST to learn about new releases, sales, behind-the-scenes trivia about the book characters, pictures of Nyx's pets, and links to insightful and often hilarious *From the Cauldron With Godfrey blog*!

DEAR MAGICKAL READER,

I hope you enjoyed this story! If you did, and would be so kind, would you leave a review on Goodreads, Bookbub, or your favorite book retailer? I would REALLY appreciate it!

A review lets hundreds, if not thousands, of potential readers know what you enjoyed about the book, and helps them make wise buying choices.

The review doesn't have to be anything long! Pretend you're sharing the story with a good friend. Pick out one or more characters, scenes, or dialogue that made you smile, laugh, or warmed your heart, and tell them about it. Just a few sentences is perfect!

Blessed be,

Nyx 🤍